The Body in the Library

**Center Point
Large Print**

Also available from Center Point Large Print
in the Miss Marple Mystery Series:

The Murder at the Vicarage

**This Large Print Book carries the
Seal of Approval of N.A.V.H.**

Agatha Christie

The Body in the Library

A Miss Marple Mystery

CENTER POINT PUBLISHING
THORNDIKE, MAINE

This Center Point Large Print edition is published in the year 2011 by arrangement with Harper Paperbacks, an imprint of HarperCollins Publishers.

The Body in the Library was first published in 1942. Published by permission of G. P. Putnam's Sons, a member of Penguin Group (USA) Inc. All rights reserved.

The text of this Large Print edition is unabridged. In other aspects, this book may vary from the original edition. Printed in the United States of America on permanent paper. Set in 16-point Times New Roman type.

ISBN: 978-1-61173-155-2

Library of Congress Cataloging-in-Publication Data

Christie, Agatha, 1890–1976.
The body in the library : a Miss Marple mystery / Agatha Christie.
  p. cm.
ISBN 978-1-61173-155-2 (library binding : alk. paper)
1. Marple, Jane (Fictitious character)—Fiction.
   2. Women detectives—England—Fiction. 3. Large type books. I. Title.
PR6005.H66B7 2011
823'.912—dc22

                                                        2011014109

To My Friend Nan

Foreword

There are certain clichés belonging to certain types of fiction. The "bold bad baronet" for melodrama, the "body in the library" for the detective story. For several years I treasured up the possibility of a suitable "Variation on a well-known Theme." I laid down for myself certain conditions. The library in question must be a highly orthodox and conventional library. The body, on the other hand, must be a wildly improbable and highly sensational body. Such were the terms of the problem, but for some years they remained as such, represented only by a few lines of writing in an exercise book. Then, staying one summer for a few days at a fashionable hotel by the seaside I observed a family at one of the tables in the dining room; an elderly man, a cripple, in a wheeled chair, and with him was a family party of a younger generation. Fortunately they left the next day, so that my imagination could get to work unhampered by any kind of knowledge. When people ask "Do you put real people in your books?" the answer is that, for me, it is quite impossible to write about anyone I know, or have ever spoken to, or indeed have even heard about! For some reason, it kills them for me stone dead. But I can take a "lay figure" and endow it with qualities and imaginings of my own.

So an elderly crippled man became the pivot of the story. Colonel and Mrs. Bantry, those old cronies of my Miss Marple, had just the right kind of library. In the manner of a cookery recipe add the following ingredients: a tennis pro, a young dancer, an artist, a girl guide, a dance hostess, etc., and serve up *à la* Miss Marple!

Agatha Christie

One

Mrs. Bantry was dreaming. Her sweet peas had just taken a First at the flower show. The vicar, dressed in cassock and surplice, was giving out the prizes in church. His wife wandered past, dressed in a bathing suit, but as is the blessed habit of dreams this fact did not arouse the disapproval of the parish in the way it would assuredly have done in real life. . . .

Mrs. Bantry was enjoying her dream a good deal. She usually did enjoy those early-morning dreams that were terminated by the arrival of early-morning tea. Somewhere in her inner consciousness was an awareness of the usual early-morning noises of the household. The rattle of the curtain rings on the stairs as the housemaid drew them, the noises of the second housemaid's dustpan and brush in the passage outside. In the distance the heavy noise of the front-door bolt being drawn back.

Another day was beginning. In the meantime she must extract as much pleasure as possible from the flower show—for already its dream-like quality was becoming apparent. . . .

Below her was the noise of the big wooden shutters in the drawing room being opened. She heard it, yet did not hear it. For quite half an hour longer the usual household noises would go on, discreet, subdued, not disturbing because they were so familiar. They would culminate in a swift, controlled sound of footsteps along the passage, the rustle of a print dress, the subdued chink of tea things as the tray was deposited on the table outside, then the soft knock and the entry of Mary to draw the curtains.

In her sleep Mrs. Bantry frowned. Something disturbing was penetrating through to the dream state, something out of its time. Footsteps along the passage, footsteps that were too hurried and too soon. Her ears listened unconsciously for the chink of china, but there was no chink of china.

The knock came at the door. Automatically from the depths of her dreams Mrs. Bantry said: "Come in." The door opened—now there would be the chink of curtain rings as the curtains were drawn back.

But there was no chink of curtain rings. Out of the dim green light Mary's voice came—breathless, hysterical: "Oh, ma'am, oh, ma'am, *there's a body in the library.*"

And then with a hysterical burst of sobs she rushed out of the room again.

II

Mrs. Bantry sat up in bed.

Either her dream had taken a very odd turn or else—or else Mary had really rushed into the

10

room and had said (incredible! fantastic!) that there was a body in the library.

"Impossible," said Mrs. Bantry to herself. "I must have been dreaming."

But even as she said it, she felt more and more certain that she had not been dreaming, that Mary, her superior self-controlled Mary, had actually uttered those fantastic words.

Mrs. Bantry reflected a minute and then applied an urgent conjugal elbow to her sleeping spouse.

"Arthur, Arthur, wake up."

Colonel Bantry grunted, muttered, and rolled over on his side.

"Wake up, Arthur. Did you hear what she said?"

"Very likely," said Colonel Bantry indistinctly. "I quite agree with you, Dolly," and promptly went to sleep again.

Mrs. Bantry shook him.

"You've got to listen. Mary came in and said that there was a body in the library."

"Eh, what?"

"A *body* in the *library*."

"Who said so?"

"Mary."

Colonel Bantry collected his scattered faculties and proceeded to deal with the situation. He said:

"Nonsense, old girl; you've been dreaming."

"No, I haven't. I thought so, too, at first. But I haven't. She really came in and said so."

"Mary came in and said there was a body in the library?"

"Yes."

"But there couldn't be," said Colonel Bantry.

"No, no, I suppose not," said Mrs. Bantry doubtfully.

Rallying, she went on:

"But then why did Mary say there was?"

"She can't have."

"She did."

"You must have imagined it."

"I didn't imagine it."

Colonel Bantry was by now thoroughly awake and prepared to deal with the situation on its merits. He said kindly:

"You've been dreaming, Dolly, that's what it is. It's that detective story you were reading—*The Clue of the Broken Match*. You know—Lord Edgbaston finds a beautiful blonde dead on the library hearthrug. Bodies are always being found in libraries in books. I've never known a case in real life."

"Perhaps you will now," said Mrs. Bantry. "Anyway, Arthur, you've got to get up and see."

"But really, Dolly, it *must* have been a dream. Dreams often do seem wonderfully vivid when you first wake up. You feel quite sure they're true."

"I was having quite a different sort of dream—about a flower show and the vicar's wife in a bathing dress—something like that."

With a sudden burst of energy Mrs. Bantry jumped out of bed and pulled back the curtains. The light of a fine autumn day flooded the room.

"I did *not* dream it," said Mrs. Bantry firmly. "Get up at once, Arthur, and go downstairs and see about it."

"You want me to go downstairs and ask if there's a body in the library? I shall look a damned fool."

"You needn't ask anything," said Mrs. Bantry. "If there *is* a body—and of course it's just possible that Mary's gone mad and thinks she sees things that aren't there—well, somebody will tell you soon enough. *You* won't have to say a word."

Grumbling, Colonel Bantry wrapped himself in his dressing gown and left the room. He went along the passage and down the staircase. At the foot of it was a little knot of huddled servants; some of them were sobbing. The butler stepped forward impressively.

"I'm glad you have come, sir. I have directed that nothing should be done until you came. Will it be in order for me to ring up the police, sir?"

"Ring 'em up about what?"

The butler cast a reproachful glance over his shoulder at the tall young woman who was weeping hysterically on the cook's shoulder.

"I understood, sir, that Mary had already informed you. She said she had done so."

Mary gasped out:

"I was so upset I don't know what I said. It all came over me again and my legs gave way and my inside turned over. Finding it like that—oh, oh, oh!"

She subsided again on to Mrs. Eccles, who said: "There, there, my dear," with some relish.

"Mary is naturally somewhat upset, sir, having been the one to make the gruesome discovery," explained the butler. "She went into the library as usual, to draw the curtains, and—almost stumbled over the body."

"Do you mean to tell me," demanded Colonel Bantry, "that there's a dead body in my library— *my* library?"

The butler coughed.

"Perhaps, sir, you would like to see for yourself."

III

"Hallo, 'allo, 'allo. Police station here. Yes, who's speaking?"

Police-Constable Palk was buttoning up his tunic with one hand while the other held the receiver.

"Yes, yes, Gossington Hall. Yes? Oh, good morning, sir." Police-Constable Palk's tone underwent a slight modification. It became less impatiently official, recognizing the generous patron of the police sports and the principal magistrate of the district.

"Yes, sir? What can I do for you?—I'm sorry, sir, I didn't quite catch—a *body,* did you say?—yes?—yes, if you please, sir—that's right, sir—young woman not known to you, you say?—quite, sir. Yes, you can leave it all to me."

Police-Constable Palk replaced the receiver, uttered a long-drawn whistle and proceeded to dial his superior officer's number.

Mrs. Palk looked in from the kitchen whence proceeded an appetizing smell of frying bacon.

"What is it?"

"Rummest thing you ever heard of," replied her husband. "Body of a young woman found up at the Hall. In the Colonel's library."

"Murdered?"

"Strangled, so he says."

"Who was she?"

"The Colonel says he doesn't know her from Adam."

"Then what was she doing in 'is library?"

Police-Constable Palk silenced her with a reproachful glance and spoke officially into the telephone.

"Inspector Slack? Police-Constable Palk here. A report has just come in that the body of a young woman was discovered this morning at seven-fifteen—"

IV

Miss Marple's telephone rang when she was dressing. The sound of it flurried her a little. It was an unusual hour for her telephone to ring. So well ordered was her prim spinster's life that unforeseen telephone calls were a source of vivid conjecture.

"Dear me," said Miss Marple, surveying the ringing instrument with perplexity. "I wonder who that can be?"

Nine o'clock to nine-thirty was the recognized time for the village to make friendly calls to neighbours. Plans for the day, invitations and so on were always issued then. The butcher had been known to ring up just before nine if some crisis in the meat trade had occurred. At intervals during the day spasmodic calls might occur, though it was considered bad form to ring after nine-thirty at night. It was true that Miss Marple's nephew, a writer, and therefore erratic, had been known to ring up at the most peculiar times, once as late as ten minutes to midnight. But whatever Raymond West's eccentricities, early rising was not one of them. Neither he nor anyone of Miss Marple's acquaintance would be likely to ring up before eight in the morning. Actually a quarter to eight.

Too early even for a telegram, since the post office did not open until eight.

"It must be," Miss Marple decided, "a wrong number."

Having decided this, she advanced to the impatient instrument and quelled its clamour by picking up the receiver. "Yes?" she said.

"Is that you, Jane?"

Miss Marple was much surprised.

"Yes, it's Jane. You're up very early, Dolly."

Mrs. Bantry's voice came breathless and agitated over the wires.

"The most awful thing has happened."

"Oh, my dear."

"We've just found a body in the library."

For a moment Miss Marple thought her friend had gone mad.

"You've found a *what?*"

"I know. One doesn't believe it, does one? I mean, I thought they only happened in books. I had to argue for hours with Arthur this morning before he'd even go down and see."

Miss Marple tried to collect herself. She demanded breathlessly: "But whose body is it?"

"It's a blonde."

"A what?"

"A blonde. A beautiful blonde—like books again. None of us have ever seen her before. She's just lying there in the library, dead. That's why you've got to come up at once."

"You want *me* to come up?"

"Yes, I'm sending the car down for you."

Miss Marple said doubtfully:

"Of course, dear, if you think I can be of any comfort to you—"

"Oh, I don't want comfort. But you're so good at bodies."

"Oh no, indeed. My little successes have been mostly theoretical."

"But you're very good at murders. She's been murdered, you see, strangled. What I feel is that if one has got to have a murder actually happening in one's house, one might as well enjoy it, if you know what I mean. That's why I want you to come and help me find out who did it and unravel the mystery and all that. It really *is* rather thrilling, isn't it?"

"Well, of course, my dear, if I can be of any *help* to you."

"Splendid! Arthur's being rather difficult. He seems to think I shouldn't enjoy myself about it at all. Of course, I do know it's very sad and all that, but then I don't know the girl—and when you've seen her you'll understand what I mean when I say she doesn't look *real* at all."

V

A little breathless, Miss Marple alighted from the Bantry's car, the door of which was held open for her by the chauffeur.

Colonel Bantry came out on the steps, and looked a little surprised.

"Miss Marple?—er—very pleased to see you."

"Your wife telephoned to me," explained Miss Marple.

"Capital, capital. She ought to have someone with her. She'll crack up otherwise. She's putting a good face on things at the moment, but you know what it is—"

At this moment Mrs. Bantry appeared, and exclaimed:

"Do go back into the dining room and eat your breakfast, Arthur. Your bacon will get cold."

"I thought it might be the Inspector arriving," explained Colonel Bantry.

"He'll be here soon enough," said Mrs. Bantry. "That's why it's important to get your breakfast first. You need it."

"So do you. Much better come and eat something. Dolly—"

"I'll come in a minute," said Mrs. Bantry. "Go on, Arthur."

Colonel Bantry was shooed back into the dining room like a recalcitrant hen.

"Now!" said Mrs. Bantry with an intonation of triumph. "Come on."

She led the way rapidly along the long corridor to the east of the house. Outside the library door Constable Palk stood on guard. He intercepted Mrs. Bantry with a show of authority.

"I'm afraid nobody is allowed in, madam. Inspector's orders."

"Nonsense, Palk," said Mrs. Bantry. "You know Miss Marple perfectly well."

Constable Palk admitted to knowing Miss Marple.

"It's very important that she should see the body," said Mrs. Bantry. "Don't be stupid, Palk. After all, it's *my* library, isn't it?"

Constable Palk gave way. His habit of giving in to the gentry was lifelong. The Inspector, he reflected, need never know about it.

"Nothing must be touched or handled in any way," he warned the ladies.

"Of course not," said Mrs. Bantry impatiently. "We know *that.* You can come in and watch, if you like."

Constable Palk availed himself of this permission. It had been his intention, anyway.

Mrs. Bantry bore her friend triumphantly across the library to the big old-fashioned fireplace. She said, with a dramatic sense of climax: "There!"

Miss Marple understood then just what her friend had meant when she said the dead girl wasn't real. The library was a room very typical of its owners. It was large and shabby and untidy. It had big sagging armchairs, and pipes and books and estate papers laid out on the big table. There were one or two good old family portraits on the walls, and some bad Victorian watercolours, and some would-be-funny hunting scenes. There was a big vase of Michaelmas daisies in the corner. The whole room was dim and mellow and casual. It spoke of long occupation and familiar use and of links with tradition.

And across the old bearskin hearthrug there was sprawled something new and crude and melodramatic.

The flamboyant figure of a girl. A girl with unnaturally fair hair dressed up off her face in elaborate curls and rings. Her thin body was dressed in a backless evening dress of white spangled satin. The face was heavily made-up, the powder standing out grotesquely on its blue swollen surface, the mascara of the lashes lying thickly on the distorted cheeks, the scarlet of the lips looking like a gash. The fingernails were enamelled in a deep blood-red and so were the toenails in their cheap silver sandal shoes. It was a cheap, tawdry, flamboyant figure—most incongruous in the solid old-fashioned comfort of Colonel Bantry's library.

Mrs. Bantry said in a low voice:

"You see what I mean? It just isn't *true!*"

The old lady by her side nodded her head. She looked down long and thoughtfully at the huddled figure.

She said at last in a gentle voice:

"She's very young."

"Yes—yes—I suppose she is." Mrs. Bantry

seemed almost surprised—like one making a discovery.

Miss Marple bent down. She did not touch the girl. She looked at the fingers that clutched frantically at the front of the girl's dress, as though she had clawed it in her last frantic struggle for breath.

There was the sound of a car scrunching on the gravel outside. Constable Palk said with urgency:

"That'll be the Inspector. . . ."

True to his ingrained belief that the gentry didn't let you down, Mrs. Bantry immediately moved to the door. Miss Marple followed her. Mrs. Bantry said:

"That'll be all right, Palk."

Constable Palk was immensely relieved.

VI

Hastily downing the last fragments of toast and marmalade with a drink of coffee, Colonel Bantry hurried out into the hall and was relieved to see Colonel Melchett, the Chief Constable of the county, descending from a car with Inspector Slack in attendance. Melchett was a friend of the Colonel's. Slack he had never much taken to—an energetic man who belied his name and who accompanied his bustling manner with a good deal of disregard for the feelings of anyone he did not consider important.

"Morning, Bantry," said the Chief Constable. "Thought I'd better come along myself. This seems an extraordinary business."

"It's—it's—" Colonel Bantry struggled to express himself. "It's *incredible—fantastic!*"

"No idea who the woman is?"

"Not the slightest. Never set eyes on her in my life."

"Butler know anything?" asked Inspector Slack.

"Lorrimer is just as taken aback as I am."

"Ah," said Inspector Slack. "I wonder."

Colonel Bantry said:

"There's breakfast in the dining room, Melchett, if you'd like anything?"

"No, no—better get on with the job. Haydock ought to be here any minute now—ah, here he is."

Another car drew up and big, broad-shouldered Doctor Haydock, who was also the police surgeon, got out. A second police car had disgorged two plainclothes men, one with a camera.

"All set—eh?" said the Chief Constable. "Right. We'll go along. In the library, Slack tells me."

Colonel Bantry groaned.

"It's incredible! You know, when my wife insisted this morning that the housemaid had come in and said there was a body in the library, I just wouldn't believe her."

"No, no, I can quite understand that. Hope your missus isn't too badly upset by it all?"

"She's been wonderful—really wonderful. She's got old Miss Marple up here with her—from the village, you know."

"Miss Marple?" The Chief Constable stiffened. "Why did she send for her?"

"Oh, a woman wants another woman—don't you think so?"

Colonel Melchett said with a slight chuckle:

"If you ask me, your wife's going to try her hand at a little amateur detecting. Miss Marple's quite the local sleuth. Put it over us properly once, didn't she, Slack?"

Inspector Slack said: "That was different."

"Different from what?"

"That was a local case, that was, sir. The old lady knows everything that goes on in the village, that's true enough. But she'll be out of her depth here."

Melchett said dryly: "You don't know very much about it yourself yet, Slack."

"Ah, you wait, sir. It won't take me long to get down to it."

VII

In the dining room Mrs. Bantry and Miss Marple, in their turn, were partaking of breakfast.

After waiting on her guest, Mrs. Bantry said urgently:

"Well, Jane?"

Miss Marple looked up at her, slightly bewildered.

Mrs. Bantry said hopefully:

"Doesn't it *remind* you of anything?"

For Miss Marple had attained fame by her ability to link up trivial village happenings with graver problems in such a way as to throw light upon the latter.

"No," said Miss Marple thoughtfully, "I can't say that it does—not at the moment. I was reminded a little of Mrs. Chetty's youngest— Edie, you know—but I think that was just because this poor girl bit her nails and her front teeth stuck out a little. Nothing more than that. And, of course," went on Miss Marple, pursuing the parallel further, "Edie was fond of what I call cheap finery, too."

"You mean her dress?" said Mrs. Bantry.

"Yes, a very tawdry satin—poor quality."

Mrs. Bantry said:

"I know. One of those nasty little shops where everything is a guinea." She went on hopefully:

"Let me see, what happened to Mrs. Chetty's Edie?"

"She's just gone into her second place—and doing very well, I believe."

Mrs. Bantry felt slightly disappointed. The village parallel didn't seem to be exactly hopeful.

"What I can't make out," said Mrs. Bantry, "is

what she could possibly be doing in Arthur's study. The window was forced, Palk tells me. She might have come down here with a burglar and then they quarrelled—but that seems such nonsense, doesn't it?"

"She was hardly dressed for burglary," said Miss Marple thoughtfully.

"No, she was dressed for dancing—or a party of some kind. But there's nothing of that kind down here—or anywhere near."

"N-n-o," said Miss Marple doubtfully.

Mrs. Bantry pounced.

"Something's in your mind, Jane."

"Well, I was just wondering—"

"Yes?"

"Basil Blake."

Mrs. Bantry cried impulsively: "Oh, no!" and added as though in explanation, "I know his mother."

The two women looked at each other.

Miss Marple sighed and shook her head.

"I quite understand how you feel about it."

"Selina Blake is the nicest woman imaginable. Her herbaceous borders are simply marvellous— they make me green with envy. And she's frightfully generous with cuttings."

Miss Marple, passing over these claims to consideration on the part of Mrs. Blake, said:

"All the same, you know, there has been a lot of *talk*."

"Oh, I know—I know. And of course Arthur goes simply livid when he hears Basil Blake mentioned. He was really *very* rude to Arthur, and since then Arthur won't hear a good word for him. He's got that silly slighting way of talking that these boys have nowadays—sneering at people sticking up for their school or the Empire or that sort of thing. And then, of course, the *clothes* he wears!

"People say," continued Mrs. Bantry, "that it doesn't matter what you wear in the country. I never heard such nonsense. It's just in the country that everyone notices." She paused, and added wistfully: "He was an adorable baby in his bath."

"There was a lovely picture of the Cheviot murderer as a baby in the paper last Sunday," said Miss Marple.

"Oh, but Jane, you don't think *he*—"

"No, no, dear. I didn't mean that at all. That would indeed be jumping to conclusions. I was just trying to account for the young woman's presence down here. St. Mary Mead is such an unlikely place. And then it seemed to me that the only possible explanation was Basil Blake. He *does* have parties. People came down from London and from the studios—you remember last July? Shouting and singing—the most *terrible* noise—everyone very drunk, I'm afraid—and the mess and the broken glass next morning simply unbelievable—so old Mrs. Berry told me—and a young woman asleep in the bath with practically *nothing on!*"

Mrs. Bantry said indulgently:

"I suppose they were film people."

"Very likely. And then—what I expect you've heard—several weekends lately he's brought down a young woman with him—a platinum blonde."

Mrs. Bantry exclaimed:

"You don't think it's *this* one?"

"Well—I wondered. Of course, I've never seen her close to—only just getting in and out of the car—and once in the cottage garden when she was sunbathing with just some shorts and a brassière. I never really saw her *face.* And all these girls with their makeup and their hair and their nails look so alike."

"Yes. Still, it *might* be. It's an idea, Jane."

Two

It was an idea that was being at that moment discussed by Colonel Melchett and Colonel Bantry.

The Chief Constable, after viewing the body and seeing his subordinates set to work on their routine tasks, had adjourned with the master of the house to the study in the other wing of the house.

Colonel Melchett was an irascible-looking man with a habit of tugging at his short red moustache. He did so now, shooting a perplexed sideways glance at the other man. Finally, he rapped out:

"Look here, Bantry, got to get this off my chest. Is it a fact that you don't know from Adam who this girl is?"

The other's answer was explosive, but the Chief Constable interrupted him.

"Yes, yes, old man, but look at it like this. Might be deuced awkward for you. Married man—fond of your missus and all that. But just between ourselves—if you *were* tied up with this girl in any way, better say so *now*. Quite natural to want to suppress the fact—should feel the same myself. But it won't do. Murder case. Facts bound to come out. Dash it all, I'm not suggesting *you* strangled the girl—not the sort of thing you'd do—*I* know that. But, after all, she came here—

29

to this house. Put it she broke in and was waiting to see you, and some bloke or other followed her down and did her in. Possible, you know. See what I mean?"

"Damn it all, Melchett, I tell you I've never set eyes on that girl in my life! I'm not that sort of man."

"That's all right, then. Shouldn't blame you, you know. Man of the world. Still, if you say so— Question is, what was she doing down here? She doesn't come from these parts—that's quite certain."

"The whole thing's a nightmare," fumed the angry master of the house.

"The point is, old man, what was she doing in your library?"

"How should I know? *I* didn't ask her here."

"No, no. But she *came* here, all the same. Looks as though she wanted to see you. You haven't had any odd letters or anything?"

"No, I haven't."

Colonel Melchett inquired delicately:

"What were you doing yourself last night?"

"I went to the meeting of the Conservative Association. Nine o'clock, at Much Benham."

"And you got home when?"

"I left Much Benham just after ten—had a bit of trouble on the way home, had to change a wheel. I got back at a quarter to twelve."

"You didn't go into the library?"

"No."

"Pity."

"I was tired. I went straight up to bed."

"Anyone waiting up for you?"

"No. I always take the latchkey. Lorrimer goes to bed at eleven unless I give orders to the contrary."

"Who shuts up the library?"

"Lorrimer. Usually about seven-thirty this time of year."

"Would he go in there again during the evening?"

"Not with my being out. He left the tray with whisky and glasses in the hall."

"I see. What about your wife?"

"I don't know. She was in bed when I got home and fast asleep. She may have sat in the library yesterday evening or in the drawing room. I forgot to ask her."

"Oh well, we shall soon know all the details. Of course, it's possible one of the servants may be concerned, eh?"

Colonel Bantry shook his head.

"I don't believe it. They're all a most respectable lot. We've had 'em for years."

Melchett agreed.

"Yes, it doesn't seem likely that they're mixed up in it. Looks more as though the girl came down from town—perhaps with some young fellow. Though why they wanted to break into this house—"

Bantry interrupted.

"London. That's more like it. We don't have goings on down here—at least—"

"Well, what is it?"

"Upon my word!" exploded Colonel Bantry. "Basil Blake!"

"Who's he?"

"Young fellow connected with the film industry. Poisonous young brute. My wife sticks up for him because she was at school with his mother, but of all the decadent useless young jackanapes! Wants his behind kicked! He's taken that cottage on the Lansham Road—you know—ghastly modern bit of building. He has parties there, shrieking, noisy crowds, and he has girls down for the weekend."

"Girls?"

"Yes, there was one last week—one of these platinum blondes—"

The Colonel's jaw dropped.

"A platinum blonde, eh?" said Melchett reflectively.

"Yes. I say, Melchett, you don't think—"

The Chief Constable said briskly:

"It's a possibility. It accounts for a girl of this type being in St. Mary Mead. I think I'll run along and have a word with this young fellow—Braid—Blake—what did you say his name was?"

"Blake. Basil Blake."

"Will he be at home, do you know?"

"Let me see. What's today—Saturday? Usually gets here sometime Saturday morning."

Melchett said grimly:

"We'll see if we can find him."

II

Basil Blake's cottage, which consisted of all modern conveniences enclosed in a hideous shell of half timbering and sham Tudor, was known to the postal authorities, and to William Booker, builder, as "Chatsworth"; to Basil and his friends as "The Period Piece," and to the village of St. Mary Mead at large as "Mr. Booker's new house."

It was little more than a quarter of a mile from the village proper, being situated on a new building estate that had been bought by the enterprising Mr. Booker just beyond the Blue Boar, with frontage on what had been a particularly unspoilt country lane. Gossington Hall was about a mile farther on along the same road.

Lively interest had been aroused in St. Mary Mead when news went round that "Mr. Booker's new house" had been bought by a film star. Eager watch was kept for the first appearance of the legendary creature in the village, and it may be said that as far as appearances went Basil

Blake was all that could be asked for. Little by little, however, the real facts leaked out. Basil Blake was *not* a film star—not even a film actor. He was a very junior person, rejoicing in the title of about fifteenth in the list of those responsible for Set Decorations at Lemville Studios, headquarters of British New Era Films. The village maidens lost interest, and the ruling class of censorious spinsters took exception to Basil Blake's way of life. Only the landlord of the Blue Boar continued to be enthusiastic about Basil and Basil's friends. The revenues of the Blue Boar had increased since the young man's arrival in the place.

The police car stopped outside the distorted rustic gate of Mr. Booker's fancy, and Colonel Melchett, with a glance of distaste at the excessive half timbering of Chatsworth, strode up to the front door and attacked it briskly with the knocker.

It was opened much more promptly than he had expected. A young man with straight, somewhat long, black hair, wearing orange corduroy trousers and a royal-blue shirt, snapped out: "Well, what do you want?"

"Are you Mr. Basil Blake?"

"Of course I am."

"I should be glad to have a few words with you, if I may, Mr. Blake?"

"Who are you?"

"I am Colonel Melchett, the Chief Constable of the County."

Mr. Blake said insolently:

"You don't say so; how amusing!"

And Colonel Melchett, following the other in, understood what Colonel Bantry's reactions had been. The toe of his own boot itched.

Containing himself, however, he said with an attempt to speak pleasantly:

"You're an early riser, Mr. Blake."

"Not at all. I haven't been to bed yet."

"Indeed."

"But I don't suppose you've come here to inquire into my hours of bedgoing—or if you have it's rather a waste of the county's time and money. What is it you want to speak to me about?"

Colonel Melchett cleared his throat.

"I understand, Mr. Blake, that last weekend you had a visitor—a—er—fair-haired young lady."

Basil Blake stared, threw back his head and roared with laughter.

"Have the old cats been on to you from the village? About my morals? Damn it all, morals aren't a police matter. *You* know that."

"As you say," said Melchett dryly, "your morals are no concern of mine. I have come to you because the body of a fair-haired young woman of slightly—er—exotic appearance has been found—murdered."

"Strewth!" Blake stared at him. "Where?"

"In the library at Gossington Hall."

"At Gossington? At old Bantry's? I say, that's pretty rich. Old Bantry! The dirty old man!"

Colonel Melchett went very red in the face. He said sharply through the renewed mirth of the young man opposite him: "Kindly control your tongue, sir. I came to ask you if you can throw any light on this business."

"You've come round to ask me if I've missed a blonde? Is that it? Why should—hallo, 'allo, 'allo, what's this?"

A car had drawn up outside with a scream of brakes. Out of it tumbled a young woman dressed in flapping black-and-white pyjamas. She had scarlet lips, blackened eyelashes, and a platinum-blonde head. She strode up to the door, flung it open, and exclaimed angrily:

"Why did you run out on me, you brute?"

Basil Blake had risen.

"So there you are! Why shouldn't I leave you? I told you to clear out and you wouldn't."

"Why the hell should I because you told me to? I was enjoying myself."

"Yes—with that filthy brute Rosenberg. You know what *he's* like."

"You were jealous, that's all."

"Don't flatter yourself. I hate to see a girl I like who can't hold her drink and lets a disgusting Central European paw her about."

36

"That's a damned lie. You were drinking pretty hard yourself—and going on with the black-haired Spanish bitch."

"If I take you to a party I expect you to be able to behave yourself."

"And I refuse to be dictated to, and that's that. You said we'd go to the party and come on down here afterwards. I'm not going to leave a party before I'm ready to leave it."

"No—and that's why I left you flat. I was ready to come down here and I came. I don't hang round waiting for any fool of a woman."

"Sweet, polite person you are!"

"You seem to have followed me down all right!"

"I wanted to tell you what I thought of you!"

"If you think you can boss me, my girl, you're wrong!"

"And if you think you can order me about, you can think again!"

They glared at each other.

It was at this moment that Colonel Melchett seized his opportunity, and cleared his throat loudly.

Basil Blake swung round on him.

"Hallo, I forgot you were here. About time you took yourself off, isn't it? Let me introduce you—Dinah Lee—Colonel Blimp of the County Police. And now, Colonel, that you've seen my blonde is alive and in good condition, perhaps you'll get on with the good work concerning old Bantry's little bit of fluff. Good morning!"

Colonel Melchett said:

"I advise you to keep a civil tongue in your head, young man, or you'll let yourself in for trouble," and stumped out, his face red and wrathful.

Three

In his office at Much Benham, Colonel Melchett received and scrutinized the reports of his subordinates:

". . . so it all seems clear enough, sir," Inspector Slack was concluding: "Mrs. Bantry sat in the library after dinner and went to bed just before ten. She turned out the lights when she left the room and, presumably, no one entered the room afterwards. The servants went to bed at half-past ten and Lorrimer, after putting the drinks in the hall, went to bed at a quarter to eleven. Nobody heard anything out of the usual except the third housemaid, and she heard too much! Groans and a blood-curdling yell and sinister footsteps and I don't know what. The second housemaid who shares a room with her says the other girl slept all night through without a sound. It's those ones that make up things that cause us all the trouble."

"What about the forced window?"

"Amateur job, Simmons says; done with a common chisel—ordinary pattern—wouldn't have made much noise. Ought to be a chisel about the house but nobody can find it. Still, that's common enough where tools are concerned."

"Think any of the servants know anything?"

Rather unwillingly Inspector Slack replied:

"No, sir, I don't think they do. They all seemed

very shocked and upset. I had my suspicions of Lorrimer—reticent, he was, if you know what I mean—but I don't think there's anything in it."

Melchett nodded. He attached no importance to Lorrimer's reticence. The energetic Inspector Slack often produced that effect on people he interrogated.

The door opened and Dr. Haydock came in.

"Thought I'd look in and give you the rough gist of things."

"Yes, yes, glad to see you. Well?"

"Nothing much. Just what you'd think. Death was due to strangulation. Satin waistband of her own dress, which was passed round the neck and crossed at the back. Quite easy and simple to do. Wouldn't have needed great strength—that is, if the girl were taken by surprise. There are no signs of a struggle."

"What about time of death?"

"Say, between ten o'clock and midnight."

"You can't get nearer than that?"

Haydock shook his head with a slight grin.

"I won't risk my professional reputation. Not earlier than ten and not later than midnight."

"And your own fancy inclines to which time?"

"Depends. There was a fire in the grate—the room was warm—all that would delay rigor and cadaveric stiffening."

"Anything more you can say about her?"

"Nothing much. She was young—about

seventeen or eighteen, I should say. Rather immature in some ways but well developed muscularly. Quite a healthy specimen. She was virgo intacta, by the way."

And with a nod of his head the doctor left the room.

Melchett said to the Inspector:

"You're quite sure she'd never been seen before at Gossington?"

"The servants are positive of that. Quite indignant about it. They'd have remembered if they'd ever seen her about in the neighbourhood, they say."

"I expect they would," said Melchett. "Anyone of that type sticks out a mile round here. Look at that young woman of Blake's."

"Pity it wasn't her," said Slack; "then we should be able to get on a bit."

"It seems to me this girl must have come down from London," said the Chief Constable thoughtfully. "Don't believe there will be any local leads. In that case, I suppose, we should do well to call in the Yard. It's a case for them, not for us."

"Something must have brought her down here, though," said Slack. He added tentatively: "Seems to me, Colonel and Mrs. Bantry *must* know something—of course, I know they're friends of yours, sir—"

Colonel Melchett treated him to a cold stare. He said stiffly:

"You may rest assured that I'm taking every possibility into account. *Every* possibility." He went on: "You've looked through the list of persons reported missing, I suppose?"

Slack nodded. He produced a typed sheet.

"Got 'em here. Mrs. Saunders, reported missing a week ago, dark-haired, blue-eyed, thirty-six. 'Tisn't her—and, anyway, everyone knows except her husband that she's gone off with a fellow from Leeds—commercial. Mrs. Barnard—she's sixty-five. Pamela Reeves, sixteen, missing from her home last night, had attended Girl Guide rally, dark-brown hair in pigtail, five feet five—"

Melchett said irritably:

"Don't go on reading idiotic details, Slack. This wasn't a schoolgirl. In my opinion—"

He broke off as the telephone rang. "Hallo—yes—yes, Much Benham Police Headquarters—what? Just a minute—"

He listened, and wrote rapidly. Then he spoke again, a new tone in his voice:

"Ruby Keene, eighteen, occupation professional dancer, five feet four inches, slender, platinum-blonde hair, blue eyes, *retroussé* nose, believed to be wearing white diamanté evening dress, silver sandal shoes. Is that right? What? Yes, not a doubt of it, I should say. I'll send Slack over at once."

He rang off and looked at his subordinate with rising excitement. "We've got it, I think. That was the Glenshire Police" (Glenshire was the adjoining county). "Girl reported missing from the Majestic Hotel, Danemouth."

"Danemouth," said Inspector Slack. "That's more like it."

Danemouth was a large and fashionable watering-place on the coast not far away.

"It's only a matter of eighteen miles or so from here," said the Chief Constable. "The girl was a dance hostess or something at the Majestic. Didn't come on to do her turn last night and the management were very fed up about it. When she was still missing this morning one of the other girls got the wind up about her, or someone else did. It sounds a bit obscure. You'd better go over to Danemouth at once, Slack. Report there to Superintendent Harper, and cooperate with him."

II

Activity was always to Inspector Slack's taste. To rush off in a car, to silence rudely those people who were anxious to tell him things, to cut short conversations on the plea of urgent necessity. All this was the breath of life to Slack.

In an incredibly short time, therefore, he had arrived at Danemouth, reported at police headquarters, had a brief interview with a distracted and apprehensive hotel manager, and, leaving the latter with the doubtful comfort of—

"got to make sure it *is* the girl, first, before we start raising the wind"—was driving back to Much Benham in company with Ruby Keene's nearest relative.

He had put through a short call to Much Benham before leaving Danemouth, so the Chief Constable was prepared for his arrival, though not perhaps for the brief introduction of: "This is Josie, sir."

Colonel Melchett stared at his subordinate coldly. His feeling was that Slack had taken leave of his senses.

The young woman who had just got out of the car came to the rescue.

"That's what I'm known as professionally," she explained with a momentary flash of large, handsome white teeth. "Raymond and Josie, my partner and I call ourselves, and, of course, all the hotel know me as Josie. Josephine Turner's my real name."

Colonel Melchett adjusted himself to the situation and invited Miss Turner to sit down, meanwhile casting a swift, professional glance over her.

She was a good-looking young woman of perhaps nearer thirty than twenty, her looks depending more on skilful grooming than actual features. She looked competent and good-tempered, with plenty of common sense. She was not the type that would ever be described as glamorous, but she had nevertheless plenty of attraction. She was discreetly made-up and wore a dark tailor-made suit. Though she looked anxious and upset she was not, the Colonel decided, particularly grief-stricken.

As she sat down she said: "It seems too awful to be true. Do you really think it's Ruby?"

"That, I'm afraid, is what we've got to ask you to tell us. I'm afraid it may be rather unpleasant for you."

Miss Turner said apprehensively:

"Does she—does she—look very terrible?"

"Well—I'm afraid it may be rather a shock to you." He handed her his cigarette case and she accepted one gratefully.

"Do—do you want me to look at her right away?"

"It would be best, I think, Miss Turner. You see, it's not much good asking you questions until we're sure. Best get it over, don't you think?"

"All right."

They drove down to the mortuary.

When Josie came out after a brief visit, she looked rather sick.

"It's Ruby all right," she said shakily. "Poor kid! Goodness, I do feel queer. There isn't"—she looked round wistfully—"any gin?"

Gin was not available, but brandy was, and after gulping a little down Miss Turner regained her composure. She said frankly:

"It gives you a turn, doesn't it, seeing anything like that? Poor little Rube! What swine men are, aren't they?"

"You believe it was a man?"

Josie looked slightly taken aback.

"Wasn't it? Well, I mean—I naturally thought—"

"Any special man you were thinking of?"

She shook her head vigorously.

"No—not me. I haven't the least idea. Naturally Ruby wouldn't have let on to me if—"

"If what?"

Josie hesitated.

"Well—if she'd been—going about with anyone."

Melchett shot her a keen glance. He said no more until they were back at his office. Then he began:

"Now, Miss Turner, I want all the information you can give me."

"Yes, of course. Where shall I begin?"

"I'd like the girl's full name and address, her relationship to you and all you know about her."

Josephine Turner nodded. Melchett was confirmed in his opinion that she felt no particular grief. She was shocked and distressed but no more. She spoke readily enough.

"Her name was Ruby Keene—her professional name, that is. Her real name was Rosy Legge. Her mother was my mother's cousin. I've known her all my life, but not particularly well, if you know what I mean. I've got a lot of cousins—some in business, some on the stage. Ruby was more or less training for a dancer. She had some good engagements last year in panto and that sort of thing. Not really classy, but good provincial companies. Since then she's been engaged as one of the dancing partners at the Palais de Danse in Brixwell—South London. It's a nice respectable place and they look after the girls well, but there isn't much money in it." She paused.

Colonel Melchett nodded.

"Now this is where I come in. I've been dance and bridge hostess at the Majestic in Danemouth for three years. It's a good job, well paid and pleasant to do. You look after people when they arrive—size them up, of course—some like to be left alone and others are lonely and want to get into the swing of things. You try to get the right people together for bridge and all that, and get the young people dancing with each other. It needs a bit of tact and experience."

Again Melchett nodded. He thought that this girl would be good at her job; she had a pleasant, friendly way with her and was, he thought, shrewd without being in the least intellectual.

"Besides that," continued Josie, "I do a couple of exhibition dances every evening with Raymond. Raymond Starr—he's the tennis and dancing pro. Well, as it happens, this summer I slipped on the rocks bathing one day and gave my ankle a nasty turn."

Melchett had noticed that she walked with a slight limp.

"Naturally that put the stop to dancing for a bit and it was rather awkward. I didn't want the hotel to get someone else in my place. That's always a danger"—for a minute her good-natured blue eyes were hard and sharp; she was the female fighting for existence—"that they may queer your pitch, you see. So I thought of Ruby and suggested to the manager that I should get her down. I'd carry on with the hostess business and the bridge and all that. Ruby would just take on the dancing. Keep it in the family, if you see what I mean?"

Melchett said he saw.

"Well, they agreed, and I wired to Ruby and she came down. Rather a chance for her. Much better class than anything she'd ever done before. That was about a month ago."

Colonel Melchett said:

"I understand. And she was a success?"

"Oh, yes," Josie said carelessly, "she went down quite well. She doesn't dance as well as I do, but Raymond's clever and carried her through, and she was quite nice-looking, you know—slim and fair and baby-looking. Overdid the makeup a bit—I was always on at her about that. But you know what girls are. She was only eighteen, and at that age they always go and overdo it. It doesn't do for a good-class place like the Majestic. I was always ticking her off about it and getting her to tone it down."

Melchett asked: "People liked her?"

"Oh, yes. Mind you, Ruby hadn't got much comeback. She was a bit dumb. She went down better with the older men than with the young ones."

"Had she got any special friend?"

The girl's eyes met his with complete understanding.

"Not in the way *you* mean. Or, at any rate, not that *I* knew about. But then, you see, she wouldn't tell me."

Just for a moment Melchett wondered why not—Josie did not give the impression of being a strict disciplinarian. But he only said: "Will you describe to me now when you last saw your cousin."

"Last night. She and Raymond do two exhibition dances—one at 10:30 and the other at midnight. They finished the first one. After it, I noticed Ruby dancing with one of the young men staying in the hotel. I was playing bridge with some people in the lounge. There's a glass panel between the lounge and the ballroom. That's the last time I saw her. Just after midnight Raymond came up in a terrible taking, said where was Ruby, she hadn't turned up, and it was time to begin. I *was* vexed, I can tell you! That's the sort of silly thing girls do and get the management's backs up and then they get the sack! I went up with him to her room, but she wasn't there. I noticed that she'd changed. The dress she'd been dancing in—a sort of pink, foamy thing with full skirts—was lying over a chair. Usually she kept the same dress on unless it was the special dance night—Wednesdays, that is.

"I'd no idea where she'd got to. We got the band to play one more foxtrot—still no Ruby, so I said to Raymond *I'd* do the exhibition dance with him. We chose one that was easy on my ankle and made it short—but it played up my ankle pretty badly all the same. It's all swollen this morning. Still Ruby didn't show up. We sat about waiting up for her until two o'clock. Furious with her, I was."

Her voice vibrated slightly. Melchett caught the note of real anger in it. Just for a moment he wondered. The reaction seemed a little more intense than was justified by the facts. He had a feeling of something deliberately left unsaid. He said:

"And this morning, when Ruby Keene had not returned and her bed had not been slept in, you went to the police?"

He knew from Slack's brief telephone message from Danemouth that that was not the case. But he wanted to hear what Josephine Turner would say.

She did not hesitate. She said: "No, *I* didn't."

50

"Why not, Miss Turner?"

Her eyes met his frankly. She said:

"*You* wouldn't—in my place!"

"You think not?"

Josie said:

"I've got my job to think about. The one thing a hotel doesn't want is scandal—especially anything that brings in the police. I didn't think anything had happened to Ruby. Not for a minute! I thought she'd just made a fool of herself about some young man. I thought she'd turn up all right—and I was going to give her a good dressing down when she did! Girls of eighteen are such fools."

Melchett pretended to glance through his notes.

"Ah, yes, I see it was a Mr. Jefferson who went to the police. One of the guests staying at the hotel?"

Josephine Turner said shortly:

"Yes."

Colonel Melchett asked:

"What made this Mr. Jefferson do that?"

Josie was stroking the cuff of her jacket. There was a constraint in her manner. Again Colonel Melchett had a feeling that something was being withheld. She said rather sullenly:

"He's an invalid. He—he gets all het up rather easily. Being an invalid, I mean."

Melchett passed on from that. He asked:

"Who was the young man with whom you last saw your cousin dancing?"

"His name's Bartlett. He'd been there about ten days."

"Were they on very friendly terms?"

"Not specially, I should say. Not that *I* knew, anyway."

Again a curious note of anger in her voice.

"What does he have to say?"

"Said that after their dance Ruby went upstairs to powder her nose."

"That was when she changed her dress?"

"I suppose so."

"And that is the last thing you know? After that she just—"

"Vanished," said Josie. "That's right."

"Did Miss Keene know anybody in St. Mary Mead? Or in this neighbourhood?"

"I don't know. She may have done. You see, quite a lot of young men come into Danemouth to the Majestic from all round about. I wouldn't know where they lived unless they happened to mention it."

"Did you ever hear your cousin mention Gossington?"

"Gossington?" Josie looked patently puzzled.

"Gossington Hall."

She shook her head.

"Never heard of it." Her tone carried conviction. There was curiosity in it too.

"Gossington Hall," explained Colonel Melchett, "is where her body was found."

"Gossington Hall?" She stared. "How extraordinary!"

Melchett thought to himself: "Extraordinary's the word!" Aloud he said:

"Do you know a Colonel or Mrs. Bantry?"

Again Josie shook her head.

"Or a Mr. Basil Blake?"

She frowned slightly.

"I think I've heard that name. Yes, I'm sure I have—but I don't remember anything about him."

The diligent Inspector Slack slid across to his superior officer a page torn from his notebook. On it was pencilled:

"Col. Bantry dined at Majestic last week."

Melchett looked up and met the Inspector's eye. The Chief Constable flushed. Slack was an industrious and zealous officer and Melchett disliked him a good deal. But he could not disregard the challenge. The Inspector was tacitly accusing him of favouring his own class—of shielding an "old school tie."

He turned to Josie.

"Miss Turner, I should like you, if you do not mind, to accompany me to Gossington Hall."

Coldly, defiantly, almost ignoring Josie's murmur of assent, Melchett's eyes met Slack's.

Four

St. Mary Mead was having the most exciting morning it had known for a long time.

Miss Wetherby, a long-nosed, acidulated spinster, was the first to spread the intoxicating information. She dropped in upon her friend and neighbour Miss Hartnell.

"Forgive me coming so early, dear, but I thought, perhaps, you mightn't have heard the *news*."

"What news?" demanded Miss Hartnell. She had a deep bass voice and visited the poor indefatigably, however hard they tried to avoid her ministrations.

"About the body in Colonel Bantry's library—a *woman's* body—"

"In Colonel Bantry's *library*?"

"Yes. Isn't it *terrible*?"

"His *poor* wife." Miss Hartnell tried to disguise her deep and ardent pleasure.

"Yes, indeed. I don't suppose she had any idea." Miss Hartnell observed censoriously:

"She thought too much about her garden and not enough about her husband. You've got to keep an eye on a man—all the time—all the time," repeated Miss Hartnell fiercely.

"I know. I know. It's really too dreadful."

"I wonder what Jane Marple will say. Do you

think she knew anything about it? She's so sharp about these things."

"Jane Marple has gone up to Gossington."

"What? This morning?"

"Very early. Before breakfast."

"But really! I do think! Well, I mean, I think that is carrying things *too* far. We all know Jane likes to poke her nose into things—but I call this indecent!"

"Oh, but Mrs. Bantry sent for her."

"Mrs. Bantry *sent* for her?"

"Well, the car came—with Muswell driving it."

"Dear me! How very peculiar. . . ."

They were silent a minute or two digesting the news.

"Whose body?" demanded Miss Hartnell.

"You know that dreadful woman who comes down with Basil Blake?"

"That terrible peroxide blonde?" Miss Hartnell was slightly behind the times. She had not yet advanced from peroxide to platinum. "The one who lies about in the garden with practically nothing on?"

"Yes, my dear. There she was—on the hearthrug—*strangled!*"

"But what do you mean—at *Gossington?*"

Miss Wetherby nodded with infinite meaning.

"Then—Colonel Bantry *too*—?"

Again Miss Wetherby nodded.

"Oh!"

There was a pause as the ladies savoured this new addition to village scandal.

"What a wicked woman!" trumpeted Miss Hartnell with righteous wrath.

"Quite, quite abandoned, I'm afraid!"

"And Colonel Bantry—such a nice quiet man—"

Miss Wetherby said zestfully:

"Those quiet ones are often the worst. Jane Marple always says so."

II

Mrs. Price Ridley was among the last to hear the news.

A rich and dictatorial widow, she lived in a large house next door to the vicarage. Her informant was her little maid Clara.

"A *woman,* you say, Clara? *Found dead on Colonel Bantry's hearthrug?*"

"Yes, mum. And they say, mum, as she hadn't anything on at all, mum, not a stitch!"

"That will do, Clara. It is not necessary to go into details."

"No, mum, and they say, mum, that at first they thought it was Mr. Blake's young lady—what comes down for the weekends with 'im to Mr. Booker's new 'ouse. But now they say it's quite a different young lady. And the fishmonger's young man, he says he'd never have believed it of

Colonel Bantry—not with him handing round the plate on Sundays and all."

"There is a lot of wickedness in the world, Clara," said Mrs. Price Ridley. "Let this be a warning to you."

"Yes, mum. Mother, she never *will* let me take a place where there's a gentleman in the 'ouse."

"That will *do,* Clara," said Mrs. Price Ridley.

III

It was only a step from Mrs. Price Ridley's house to the vicarage.

Mrs. Price Ridley was fortunate enough to find the vicar in his study.

The vicar, a gentle, middle-aged man, was always the last to hear anything.

"Such a *terrible* thing," said Mrs. Price Ridley, panting a little, because she had come rather fast. "I felt I must have your advice, your counsel about it, dear vicar."

Mr. Clement looked mildly alarmed. He said:

"Has anything happened?"

"Has anything *happened?*" Mrs. Price Ridley repeated the question dramatically. "The most terrible scandal! None of us had any idea of it. An abandoned woman, completely unclothed, strangled on Colonel Bantry's hearthrug."

The vicar stared. He said:

"You—you are feeling quite well?"

"No wonder you can't believe it! *I* couldn't at first. The hypocrisy of the man! All these years!"

"Please tell me exactly what all this is about."

Mrs. Price Ridley plunged into a full-swing narrative. When she had finished Mr. Clement said mildly:

"But there is nothing, is there, to point to Colonel Bantry's being involved in this?"

"Oh, dear vicar, you are so unworldly! But I must tell you a little story. Last Thursday—or was it the Thursday before? well, it doesn't matter—I was going up to London by the cheap day train. Colonel Bantry was in the same carriage. He looked, I thought, very abstracted. And nearly the whole way he buried himself behind *The Times*. As though, you know, he didn't want to *talk*."

The vicar nodded with complete comprehension and possible sympathy.

"At Paddington I said good-bye. He had offered to get me a taxi, but I was taking the bus down to Oxford Street—but he got into one, and I distinctly heard him tell the driver to go to— *where do you think?*"

Mr. Clement looked inquiring.

"An address in *St. John's Wood!*"

Mrs. Price Ridley paused triumphantly.

The vicar remained completely unenlightened.

"That, I consider, *proves* it," said Mrs. Price Ridley.

IV

At Gossington, Mrs. Bantry and Miss Marple were sitting in the drawing room.

"You know," said Mrs. Bantry, "I can't help feeling glad they've taken the body away. It's not *nice* to have a body in one's house."

Miss Marple nodded.

"I know, dear. I know just how you feel."

"You can't," said Mrs. Bantry; "not until you've had one. I know you had one next door once, but that's not the same thing. I only hope," she went on, "that Arthur won't take a dislike to the library. We sit there so much. What are you doing, Jane?"

For Miss Marple, with a glance at her watch, was rising to her feet.

"Well, I was thinking I'd go home. If there's nothing more I can do for you?"

"Don't go yet," said Mrs. Bantry. "The fingerprint men and the photographers and most of the police have gone, I know, but I still feel something might happen. You don't want to miss anything."

The telephone rang and she went off to answer. She returned with a beaming face. "I told you more things would happen. That was Colonel Melchett. He's bringing the poor girl's cousin along."

"I wonder why," said Miss Marple.

"Oh, I suppose, to see where it happened and all that."

"More than that, I expect," said Miss Marple.

"What do you mean, Jane?"

"Well, I think—perhaps—he might want her to meet Colonel Bantry."

Mrs. Bantry said sharply:

"To see if she recognizes him? I suppose—oh, yes, I suppose they're bound to suspect Arthur."

"I'm afraid so."

"As though Arthur could have anything to do with it!"

Miss Marple was silent. Mrs. Bantry turned on her accusingly.

"And don't quote old General Henderson—or some frightful old man who kept his housemaid—at me. Arthur isn't like that."

"No, no, of course not."

"No, but he *really* isn't. He's just—sometimes—a little silly about pretty girls who come to tennis. You know—rather fatuous and avuncular. There's no harm in it. And why shouldn't he? After all," finished Mrs. Bantry rather obscurely, "I've got the garden."

Miss Marple smiled.

"You must not worry, Dolly," she said.

"No, I don't mean to. But all the same I do a little. So does Arthur. It's upset him. All these policemen prowling about. He's gone down to the farm. Looking at pigs and things always soothes him if he's been upset. Hallo, here they are."

The Chief Constable's car drew up outside.

Colonel Melchett came in accompanied by a smartly dressed young woman.

"This is Miss Turner, Mrs. Bantry. The cousin of the—er—victim."

"How do you do," said Mrs. Bantry, advancing with outstretched hand. "All this must be rather awful for you."

Josephine Turner said frankly: "Oh, it is. None of it seems *real,* somehow. It's like a bad dream."

Mrs. Bantry introduced Miss Marple.

Melchett said casually: "Your good man about?"

"He had to go down to one of the farms. He'll be back soon."

"Oh—" Melchett seemed rather at a loss.

Mrs. Bantry said to Josie: "Would you like to see where—where it happened? Or would you rather not?"

Josephine said after a moment's pause:

"I think I'd like to see."

Mrs. Bantry led her to her library with Miss Marple and Melchett following behind.

"She was there," said Mrs. Bantry, pointing dramatically; "on the hearthrug."

"Oh!" Josie shuddered. But she also looked perplexed. She said, her brow creased: "I just *can't* understand it! I *can't!*"

"Well, *we* certainly can't," said Mrs. Bantry.

Josie said slowly:

"It isn't the sort of place—" and broke off.

Miss Marple nodded her head gently in agreement with the unfinished sentiment. "That," she murmured, "is what makes it so very interesting."

"Come now, Miss Marple," said Colonel Melchett good-humouredly, "haven't you got an explanation?"

"Oh yes, I've got an *explanation*," said Miss Marple. "Quite a feasible one. But of course it's only my own *idea*. Tommy Bond," she continued, "and Mrs. Martin, our new schoolmistress. She went to wind up the clock and a frog jumped out."

Josephine Turner looked puzzled. As they all went out of the room she murmured to Mrs. Bantry: "Is the old lady a bit funny in the head?"

"Not at all," said Mrs. Bantry indignantly.

Josie said: "Sorry; I thought perhaps she thought she *was* a frog or something."

Colonel Bantry was just coming in through the side door. Melchett hailed him, and watched Josephine Turner as he introduced them to each other. But there was no sign of interest or recognition in her face. Melchett breathed a sigh of relief. Curse Slack and his insinuations!

In answer to Mrs. Bantry's questions Josie was pouring out the story of Ruby Keene's disappearance.

"Frightfully worrying for you, my dear," said Mrs. Bantry.

"I was more angry than worried," said Josie. "You see, I didn't know then that anything had happened to her."

"And yet," said Miss Marple, "you went to the police. Wasn't that—excuse me—rather *premature?*"

Josie said eagerly:

"Oh, but I didn't. That was Mr. Jefferson—"

Mrs. Bantry said: "Jefferson?"

"Yes, he's an invalid."

"Not *Conway* Jefferson? But I know him well. He's an old friend of ours. Arthur, listen—Conway Jefferson. He's staying at the Majestic, and it was he who went to the police! Isn't that a coincidence?"

Josephine Turner said:

"Mr. Jefferson was here last summer too."

"Fancy! And we never knew. I haven't seen him for a long time." She turned to Josie. "How—how is he, nowadays?"

Josie considered.

"I think he's wonderful, really—quite wonderful. Considering, I mean. He's always cheerful—always got a joke."

"Are the family there with him?"

"Mr. Gaskell, you mean? And young Mrs. Jefferson? And Peter? Oh, yes."

There was something inhibiting Josephine

Turner's usual attractive frankness of manner. When she spoke of the Jeffersons there was something not quite natural in her voice.

Mrs. Bantry said: "They're both very nice, aren't they? The young ones, I mean."

Josie said rather uncertainly:

"Oh yes—yes, they are. I—we—yes, they are, *really.*"

V

"And what," demanded Mrs. Bantry as she looked through the window at the retreating car of the Chief Constable, "did she mean by that? 'They are, *really.*' Don't you think, Jane, that there's something—"

Miss Marple fell upon the words eagerly.

"Oh, I do—indeed I do. It's quite *unmistakable!* Her manner changed *at once* when the Jeffersons were mentioned. She had seemed quite natural up to then."

"But what do you think it *is,* Jane?"

"Well, my dear, *you* know them. All I feel is that there is *something,* as you say, about them which is worrying that young woman. Another thing, did you notice that when you asked her if she wasn't anxious about the girl being missing, she said that she was *angry!* And she *looked* angry—*really* angry! That strikes me as *interesting,* you know. I have a feeling—perhaps

I'm wrong—that that's her main reaction to the fact of the girl's death. She didn't care for her, I'm sure. She's not grieving in any way. But I do think, very definitely, that the thought of that girl, Ruby Keene, makes her *angry*. And the interesting point is—*why?*"

"We'll find out!" said Mrs. Bantry. "We'll go over to Danemouth and stay at the Majestic—yes, Jane, you too. I need a change for my nerves after what has happened here. A few days at the Majestic—that's what we need. And you'll meet Conway Jefferson. He's a dear—a perfect dear. It's the saddest story imaginable. Had a son and daughter, both of whom he loved dearly. They were both married, but they still spent a lot of time at home. His wife, too, was the sweetest woman, and he was devoted to her. They were flying home one year from France and there was an accident. They were all killed: the pilot, Mrs. Jefferson, Rosamund, and Frank. Conway had both legs so badly injured they had to be amputated. And he's been wonderful—his courage, his pluck! He was a very active man and now he's a helpless cripple, but he never complains. His daughter-in-law lives with him—she was a widow when Frank Jefferson married her and she had a son by her first marriage—Peter Carmody. They both live with Conway. And Mark Gaskell, Rosamund's husband, is there too most of the time. The whole thing was the most awful tragedy."

"And now," said Miss Marple, "there's another tragedy—"

Mrs. Bantry said: "Oh yes—yes—but it's nothing to do with the Jeffersons."

"Isn't it?" said Miss Marple. "It was Mr. Jefferson who went to the police."

"So he did . . . You know, Jane, that *is* curious. . . ."

Five

Colonel Melchett was facing a much annoyed hotel manager. With him was Superintendent Harper of the Glenshire Police and the inevitable Inspector Slack—the latter rather disgruntled at the Chief Constable's wilful usurpation of the case.

Superintendent Harper was inclined to be soothing with the almost tearful Mr. Prestcott—Colonel Melchett tended towards a blunt brutality.

"No good crying over spilt milk," he said sharply. "The girl's dead—strangled. You're lucky that she wasn't strangled in your hotel. This puts the inquiry in a different county and lets your establishment down extremely lightly. But certain inquiries have got to be made, and the sooner we get on with it the better. You can trust us to be discreet and tactful. So I suggest you cut the cackle and come to the horses. Just what exactly do you know about the girl?"

"I knew nothing of her—nothing at all. Josie brought her here."

"Josie's been here some time?"

"Two years—no, three."

"And you like her?"

"Yes, Josie's a good girl—a nice girl. Competent. She gets on with people, and smoothes over differences—bridge, you know, is a touchy sort of game—" Colonel Melchett nodded feelingly. His wife was a keen but an extremely bad bridge player. Mr. Prestcott went on: "Josie was very good at calming down unpleasantnesses. She could handle people well—sort of bright and firm, if you know what I mean."

Again Melchett nodded. He knew now what it was Miss Josephine Turner had reminded him of. In spite of the makeup and the smart turnout there was a distinct touch of the nursery governess about her.

"I depend upon her," went on Mr. Prestcott. His manner became aggrieved. "What does she want to go playing about on slippery rocks in that damn' fool way? We've got a nice beach here. Why couldn't she bathe from that? Slipping and falling and breaking her ankle. It wasn't fair on *me!* I pay her to dance and play bridge and keep people happy and amused—not to go bathing off rocks and breaking her ankle. Dancers ought to be careful of their ankles—not take risks. I was very annoyed about it. It wasn't fair to the hotel."

Melchett cut the recital short.

"And then she suggested this girl—her cousin—coming down?"

Prestcott assented grudgingly.

"That's right. It sounded quite a good idea. Mind you, I wasn't going to pay anything extra.

The girl could have her keep; but as for salary, that would have to be fixed up between her and Josie. That's the way it was arranged. *I* didn't know anything about the girl."

"But she turned out all right?"

"Oh yes, there wasn't anything wrong with her—not to look at, anyway. She was very young, of course—rather cheap in style, perhaps, for a place of this kind, but nice manners—quiet and well-behaved. Danced well. People liked her."

"Pretty?"

It had been a question hard to answer from a view of the blue swollen face.

Mr. Prestcott considered.

"Fair to middling. Bit weaselly, if you know what I mean. Wouldn't have been much without makeup. As it was she managed to look quite attractive."

"Many young men hanging about after her?"

"I know what you're trying to get at, sir." Mr. Prestcott became excited. "*I* never saw anything. Nothing special. One or two of the boys hung around a bit—but all in the day's work, so to speak. Nothing in the strangling line, I'd say. She got on well with the older people, too—had a kind of prattling way with her—seemed quite a kid, if you know what I mean. It amused them."

Superintendent Harper said in a deep melancholy voice:

"Mr. Jefferson, for instance?"

The manager agreed.

"Yes, Mr. Jefferson was the one I had in mind. She used to sit with him and his family a lot. He used to take her out for drives sometimes. Mr. Jefferson's very fond of young people and very good to them. I don't want to have any misunderstanding. Mr. Jefferson's a cripple; he can't get about much—only where his wheelchair will take him. But he's always keen on seeing young people enjoy themselves—watches the tennis and the bathing and all that—and gives parties for young people here. He likes youth—and there's nothing bitter about him as there well might be. A very popular gentleman and, I'd say, a very fine character."

Melchett asked:

"And he took an interest in Ruby Keene?"

"Her talk amused him, I think."

"Did his family share his liking for her?"

"They were always very pleasant to her."

Harper said:

"And it was he who reported the fact of her being missing to the police?"

He contrived to put into the word a significance and a reproach to which the manager instantly responded.

"Put yourself in my place, Mr. Harper. *I* didn't dream for a minute anything was wrong. Mr. Jefferson came along to my office, storming, and all worked up. The girl hadn't slept in her room.

She hadn't appeared in her dance last night. She must have gone for a drive and had an accident, perhaps. The police must be informed at once! Inquiries made! In a state, he was, and quite high-handed. He rang up the police station then and there."

"Without consulting Miss Turner?"

"Josie didn't like it much. I could see that. She was very annoyed about the whole thing—annoyed with Ruby, I mean. But what could she say?"

"I think," said Melchett, "we'd better see Mr. Jefferson. Eh, Harper?"

Superintendent Harper agreed.

II

Mr. Prestcott went up with them to Conway Jefferson's suite. It was on the first floor, overlooking the sea. Melchett said carelessly:

"Does himself pretty well, eh? Rich man?"

"Very well off indeed, I believe. Nothing's ever stinted when he comes here. Best rooms reserved—food usually *à la carte,* expensive wines—best of everything."

Melchett nodded.

Mr. Prestcott tapped on the outer door and a woman's voice said: "Come in."

The manager entered, the others behind him.

Mr. Prestcott's manner was apologetic as he

spoke to the woman who turned her head at their entrance from her seat by the window.

"I am so sorry to disturb you, Mrs. Jefferson, but these gentlemen are—from the police. They are very anxious to have a word with Mr. Jefferson. Er—Colonel Melchett—Superintendent Harper, Inspector—er—Slack—Mrs. Jefferson."

Mrs. Jefferson acknowledged the introduction by bending her head.

A plain woman, was Melchett's first impression. Then, as a slight smile came to her lips and she spoke, he changed his opinion. She had a singularly charming and sympathetic voice and her eyes, clear hazel eyes, were beautiful. She was quietly but not unbecomingly dressed and was, he judged, about thirty-five years of age.

She said:

"My father-in-law is asleep. He is not strong at all, and this affair has been a terrible shock to him. We had to have the doctor, and the doctor gave him a sedative. As soon as he wakes he will, I know, want to see you. In the meantime, perhaps I can help you? Won't you sit down?"

Mr. Prestcott, anxious to escape, said to Colonel Melchett: "Well—er—if that's all I can do for you?" and thankfully received permission to depart.

With his closing of the door behind him, the atmosphere took on a mellow and more social quality. Adelaide Jefferson had the power of creating a restful atmosphere. She was a woman who never seemed to say anything remarkable but who succeeded in stimulating other people to talk and setting them at their ease. She struck now the right note when she said:

"This business has shocked us all very much. We saw quite a lot of the poor girl, you know. It seems quite unbelievable. My father-in-law is terribly upset. He was very fond of Ruby."

Colonel Melchett said:

"It was Mr. Jefferson, I understand, who reported her disappearance to the police?"

He wanted to see exactly how she would react to that. There was a flicker—just a flicker—of—annoyance? concern?—he could not say what exactly, but there was *something,* and it seemed to him she had definitely to brace herself, as though to an unpleasant task, before going on.

She said:

"Yes, that is so. Being an invalid, he gets easily upset and worried. We tried to persuade him that it was all right, that there was some natural explanation, and that the girl herself would not like the police being notified. He insisted. Well"—she made a slight gesture—"he was right and we were wrong."

Melchett asked: "Exactly how well did you know Ruby Keene, Mrs. Jefferson?"

She considered.

"It's difficult to say. My father-in-law is very

73

fond of young people and likes to have them round him. Ruby was a new type to him—he was amused and interested by her chatter. She sat with us a good deal in the hotel and my father-in-law took her out for drives in the car."

Her voice was quite noncommittal. Melchett thought to himself: "She could say more if she chose."

He said: "Will you tell me what you can of the course of events last night?"

"Certainly, but there is very little that will be useful, I'm afraid. After dinner Ruby came and sat with us in the lounge. She remained even after the dancing had started. We had arranged to play bridge later, but we were waiting for Mark, that is Mark Gaskell, my brother-in-law—he married Mr. Jefferson's daughter, you know—who had some important letters to write, and also for Josie. She was going to make a fourth with us."

"Did that often happen?"

"Quite frequently. She's a first-class player, of course, and very nice. My father-in-law is a keen bridge player and whenever possible liked to get hold of Josie to make the fourth instead of an outsider. Naturally, as she has to arrange the fours, she can't always play with us, but she does whenever she can, and as"—her eyes smiled a little—"my father-in-law spends a lot of money in the hotel, the management are quite pleased for Josie to favour us."

Melchett asked:

"You like Josie?"

"Yes, I do. She's always good-humoured and cheerful, works hard and seems to enjoy her job. She's shrewd, though not well educated, and—well—never pretends about anything. She's natural and unaffected."

"Please go on, Mrs. Jefferson."

"As I say, Josie had to get her bridge fours arranged and Mark was writing, so Ruby sat and talked with us a little longer than usual. Then Josie came along, and Ruby went off to do her first solo dance with Raymond—he's the dance and tennis professional. She came back to us afterwards just as Mark joined us. Then she went off to dance with a young man and we four started our bridge."

She stopped, and made a slight insignificant gesture of helplessness.

"And that's all I know! I just caught a glimpse of her once dancing, but bridge is an absorbing game and I hardly glanced through the glass partition at the ballroom. Then, at midnight, Raymond came along to Josie very upset and asked where Ruby was. Josie, naturally, tried to shut him up but—"

Superintendent Harper interrupted. He said in his quiet voice: "Why 'naturally,' Mrs. Jefferson?"

"Well"—she hesitated, looked, Melchett thought, a little put out—"Josie didn't want the girl's absence made too much of. She considered herself responsible for her in a way. She said Ruby was probably up in her bedroom, said the girl had talked about having a headache earlier— I don't think that was true, by the way; Josie just said it by way of excuse. Raymond went off and telephoned up to Ruby's room, but apparently there was no answer, and he came back in rather a state—temperamental, you know. Josie went off with him and tried to soothe him down, and in the end she danced with him instead of Ruby. Rather plucky of her, because you could see afterwards it had hurt her ankle. She came back to us when the dance was over and tried to calm down Mr. Jefferson. He had got worked up by then. We persuaded him in the end to go to bed, told him Ruby had probably gone for a spin in a car and that they'd had a puncture. He went to bed worried, and this morning he began to agitate at once." She paused. "The rest you know."

"Thank you, Mrs. Jefferson. Now I'm going to ask you if you've any idea who could have done this thing."

She said immediately: "No idea whatever. I'm afraid I can't help you in the slightest."

He pressed her. "The girl never said anything? Nothing about jealousy? About some man she was afraid of? Or intimate with?"

Adelaide Jefferson shook her head to each query.

There seemed nothing more that she could tell them.

The Superintendent suggested that they should interview young George Bartlett and return to see Mr. Jefferson later. Colonel Melchett agreed, and the three men went out, Mrs. Jefferson promising to send word as soon as Mr. Jefferson was awake.

"Nice woman," said the Colonel, as they closed the door behind them.

"A very nice lady indeed," said Superintendent Harper.

III

George Bartlett was a thin, lanky youth with a prominent Adam's apple and an immense difficulty in saying what he meant. He was in such a state of dither that it was hard to get a calm statement from him.

"I say, it is awful, isn't it? Sort of thing one reads about in the Sunday papers—but one doesn't feel it really happens, don't you know?"

"Unfortunately there is no doubt about it, Mr. Bartlett," said the Superintendent.

"No, no, of course not. But it seems so rum somehow. And miles from here and everything—in some country house, wasn't it? Awfully county and all that. Created a bit of a stir in the neighbourhood—what?"

Colonel Melchett took charge.

"How well did you know the dead girl, Mr. Bartlett?"

George Bartlett looked alarmed.

"Oh, n-n-n-ot well at all, s-s-sir. No, hardly at all—if you know what I mean. Danced with her once or twice—passed the time of day—bit of tennis—*you* know."

"You were, I think, the last person to see her alive last night?"

"I suppose I was—doesn't it sound awful? I mean, she was perfectly all right when I saw her—absolutely."

"What time was that, Mr. Bartlett?"

"Well, you know, I never know about time—wasn't very late, if you know what I mean."

"You danced with her?"

"Yes—as a matter of fact—well, yes, I did. Early on in the evening, though. Tell you what, it was just after her exhibition dance with the pro fellow. Must have been ten, half-past, eleven, I don't know."

"Never mind the time. We can fix that. Please tell us exactly what happened."

"Well, we danced, don't you know. Not that *I'm* much of a dancer."

"How you dance is not really relevant, Mr. Bartlett."

George Bartlett cast an alarmed eye on the Colonel and stammered:

"No—er—n-n-n-o, I suppose it isn't. Well, as I

say, we danced, round and round, and I talked, but Ruby didn't say very much and she yawned a bit. As I say, I don't dance awfully well, and so girls—well—inclined to give it a miss, if you know what I mean. She said she had a headache—I know where I get off, so I said righty ho, and that was that."

"What was the last you saw of her?"

"She went off upstairs."

"She said nothing about meeting anyone? Or going for a drive? Or—or—having a date?" The Colonel used the colloquial expression with a slight effort.

Bartlett shook his head.

"Not to me." He looked rather mournful. "Just gave me the push."

"What was her manner? Did she seem anxious, abstracted, anything on her mind?"

George Bartlett considered. Then he shook his head.

"Seemed a bit bored. Yawned, as I said. Nothing more."

Colonel Melchett said:

"And what did you do, Mr. Bartlett?"

"Eh?"

"What did you do when Ruby Keene left you?"

George Bartlett gaped at him.

"Let's see now—what *did* I do?"

"We're waiting for you to tell us."

"Yes, yes—of course. Jolly difficult,

remembering things, what? Let me see. Shouldn't be surprised if I went into the bar and had a drink."

"*Did* you go into the bar and have a drink?"

"That's just it. I *did* have a drink. Don't think it was just then. Have an idea I wandered out, don't you know? Bit of air. Rather stuffy for September. Very nice outside. Yes, that's it. I strolled around a bit, then I came in and had a drink and then I strolled back to the ballroom. Wasn't much doing. Noticed what's-her-name—Josie—was dancing again. With the tennis fellow. She'd been on the sick list—twisted ankle or something."

"That fixes the time of your return at midnight. Do you intend us to understand that you spent over an hour walking about outside?"

"Well, I had a drink, you know. I was—well, I was thinking of things."

This statement received more credulity than any other.

Colonel Melchett said sharply:

"What were you thinking about?"

"Oh, I don't know. Things," said Mr. Bartlett vaguely.

"You have a car, Mr. Bartlett?"

"Oh, yes, I've got a car."

"Where was it, in the hotel garage?"

"No, it was in the courtyard, as a matter of fact. Thought I might go for a spin, you see."

"Perhaps you did go for a spin?"

"No—no, I didn't. Swear I didn't."

"You didn't, for instance, take Miss Keene for a spin?"

"Oh, I say. Look here, what are you getting at? I didn't—I swear I didn't. Really, now."

"Thank you, Mr. Bartlett, I don't think there is anything more at present. *At present,*" repeated Colonel Melchett with a good deal of emphasis on the words.

They left Mr. Bartlett looking after them with a ludicrous expression of alarm on his unintellectual face. "Brainless young ass," said Colonel Melchett. "Or isn't he?"

Superintendent Harper shook his head.

"We've got a long way to go," he said.

Six

Neither the night porter nor the barman proved helpful. The night porter remembered ringing up to Miss Keene's room just after midnight and getting no reply. He had not noticed Mr. Bartlett leaving or entering the hotel. A lot of gentlemen and ladies were strolling in and out, the night being fine. And there were side doors off the corridor as well as the one in the main hall. He was fairly certain Miss Keene had not gone out by the main door, but if she had come down from her room, which was on the first floor, there was a staircase next to it and a door out at the end of the corridor, leading on to the side terrace. She could have gone out of that unseen easily enough. It was not locked until the dancing was over at two o'clock.

The barman remembered Mr. Bartlett being in the bar the preceding evening but could not say when. Somewhere about the middle of the evening, he thought. Mr. Bartlett had sat against the wall and was looking rather melancholy. He did not know how long he was there. There were a lot of outside guests coming and going in the bar. He had noticed Mr. Bartlett but he couldn't fix the time in any way.

II

As they left the bar, they were accosted by a small boy of about nine years old. He burst immediately into excited speech.

"I say, are you the detectives? I'm Peter Carmody. It was my grandfather, Mr. Jefferson, who rang up the police about Ruby. Are you from Scotland Yard? You don't mind my speaking to you, do you?"

Colonel Melchett looked as though he were about to return a short answer, but Superintendent Harper intervened. He spoke benignly and heartily.

"That's all right, my son. Naturally interests you, I expect?"

"You bet it does. Do you like detective stories? I do. I read them all, and I've got autographs from Dorothy Sayers and Agatha Christie and Dickson Carr and H. C. Bailey. Will the murder be in the papers?"

"It'll be in the papers all right," said Superintendent Harper grimly.

"You see, I'm going back to school next week and I shall tell them all that I knew her—really knew her *well*."

"What did you think of her, eh?"

Peter considered.

"Well, I didn't like her much. I think she was rather a stupid sort of girl. Mum and Uncle Mark didn't like her much either. Only Grandfather. Grandfather wants to see you, by the way. Edwards is looking for you."

Superintendent Harper murmured encouragingly:

"So your mother and your Uncle Mark didn't like Ruby Keene much? Why was that?"

"Oh, I don't know. She was always butting in. And they didn't like Grandfather making such a fuss of her. I expect," said Peter cheerfully, "that they're glad she's dead."

Superintendent Harper looked at him thoughtfully. He said: "Did you hear them—er—say so?"

"Well, not exactly. Uncle Mark said: 'Well, it's one way out, anyway,' and Mums said: 'Yes, but such a horrible one,' and Uncle Mark said it was no good being hypocritical."

The men exchanged glances. At that moment a respectable, clean-shaven man, neatly dressed in blue serge, came up to them.

"Excuse me, gentlemen. I am Mr. Jefferson's valet. He is awake now and sent me to find you, as he is very anxious to see you."

Once more they went up to Conway Jefferson's suite. In the sitting room Adelaide Jefferson was talking to a tall, restless man who was prowling nervously about the room. He swung round sharply to view the newcomers.

"Oh, yes. Glad you've come. My father-in-law's been asking for you. He's awake now. Keep him as calm as you can, won't you? His health's not too good. It's a wonder, really, that this shock didn't do for him."

Harper said:

"I'd no idea his health was as bad as that."

"He doesn't know it himself," said Mark Gaskell. "It's his heart, you see. The doctor warned Addie that he mustn't be overexcited or startled. He more or less hinted that the end might come any time, didn't he, Addie?"

Mrs. Jefferson nodded. She said:

"It's incredible that he's rallied the way he has."

Melchett said dryly:

"Murder isn't exactly a soothing incident. We'll be as careful as we can."

He was sizing up Mark Gaskell as he spoke. He didn't much care for the fellow. A bold, unscrupulous, hawk-like face. One of those men who usually get their own way and whom women frequently admire.

"But not the sort of fellow I'd trust," the Colonel thought to himself.

Unscrupulous—that was the word for him.

The sort of fellow who wouldn't stick at anything. . . .

III

In the big bedroom overlooking the sea, Conway Jefferson was sitting in his wheeled chair by the window.

No sooner were you in the room with him than you felt the power and magnetism of the man. It was as though the injuries which had left him a cripple had resulted in concentrating the vitality of his shattered body into a narrower and more intense focus.

He had a fine head, the red of the hair slightly grizzled. The face was rugged and powerful, deeply suntanned, and the eyes were a startling blue. There was no sign of illness or feebleness about him. The deep lines on his face were the lines of suffering, not the lines of weakness. Here was a man who would never rail against fate but accept it and pass on to victory.

He said: "I'm glad you've come." His quick eyes took them in. He said to Melchett: "You're the Chief Constable of Radfordshire? Right. And you're Superintendent Harper? Sit down. Cigarettes on the table beside you."

They thanked him and sat down. Melchett said:

"I understand, Mr. Jefferson, that you were interested in the dead girl?"

A quick, twisted smile flashed across the lined face.

"Yes—they'll all have told you that! Well, it's no secret. How much has my family said to you?"

He looked quickly from one to the other as he asked the question. It was Melchett who answered.

"Mrs. Jefferson told us very little beyond the

fact that the girl's chatter amused you and that she was by way of being a protégée. We have only exchanged half a dozen words with Mr. Gaskell."

Conway Jefferson smiled.

"Addie's a discreet creature, bless her. Mark would probably have been more outspoken. I think, Melchett, that I'd better tell you some facts rather fully. It's important, in order that you should understand my attitude. And, to begin with, it's necessary that I go back to the big tragedy of my life. Eight years ago I lost my wife, my son, and my daughter in an aeroplane accident. Since then I've been like a man who's lost half himself—and I'm not speaking of my physical plight! I was a family man. My daughter-in-law and my son-in-law have been very good to me. They've done all they can to take the place of my flesh and blood. But I've realized—especially of late, that they have, after all, their own lives to live.

"So you must understand that, essentially, I'm a lonely man. I like young people. I enjoy them. Once or twice I've played with the idea of adopting some girl or boy. During this last month I got very friendly with the child who's been killed. She was absolutely natural—completely naïve. She chattered on about her life and her experiences—in pantomime, with touring companies, with Mum and Dad as a child in cheap lodgings. Such a different life from any

I've known! Never complaining, never seeing it as sordid. Just a natural, uncomplaining, hardworking child, unspoilt and charming. Not a lady, perhaps, but, thank God, neither vulgar nor—abominable word—'lady-like.'

"I got more and more fond of Ruby. I decided, gentlemen, to adopt her legally. She would become—by law—my daughter. That, I hope, explains my concern for her and the steps I took when I heard of her unaccountable disappearance."

There was a pause. Then Superintendent Harper, his unemotional voice robbing the question of any offence, asked: "May I ask what your son-in-law and daughter-in-law said to that?"

Jefferson's answer came back quickly:

"What could they say? They didn't, perhaps, like it very much. It's the sort of thing that arouses prejudice. But they behaved very well— yes, very well. It's not as though, you see, they were dependent on me. When my son Frank married I turned over half my worldly goods to him then and there. I believe in that. Don't let your children wait until you're dead. They want the money when they're young, not when they're middle-aged. In the same way when my daughter Rosamund insisted on marrying a poor man, I settled a big sum of money on her. That sum passed to him at her death. So, you see, that simplified the matter from the financial angle."

"I see, Mr. Jefferson," said Superintendent Harper.

But there was a certain reserve in his tone. Conway Jefferson pounced upon it.

"But you don't agree, eh?"

"It's not for me to say, sir, but families, in my experience, don't always act reasonably."

"I dare say you're right, Superintendent, but you must remember that Mr. Gaskell and Mrs. Jefferson aren't, strictly speaking, my *family*. They're not blood relations."

"That, of course, makes a difference," admitted the Superintendent.

For a moment Conway Jefferson's eyes twinkled. He said: "That's not to say that they didn't think me an old fool! That *would* be the average person's reaction. But I wasn't being a fool. I know character. With education and polishing, Ruby Keene could have taken her place anywhere."

Melchett said:

"I'm afraid we're being rather impertinent and inquisitive, but it's important that we should get at all the facts. You proposed to make full provision for the girl—that is, settle money upon her, but you hadn't already done so?"

Jefferson said:

"I understand what you're driving at—the possibility of someone's benefiting by the girl's death? But nobody could. The necessary formalities for legal adoption were under way, but they hadn't yet been completed."

Melchett said slowly:

"Then, if anything happened to you—?"

He left the sentence unfinished, as a query. Conway Jefferson was quick to respond.

"Nothing's likely to happen to me! I'm a cripple, but I'm not an invalid. Although doctors *do* like to pull long faces and give advice about not overdoing things. Not overdoing things! I'm as strong as a horse! Still, I'm quite aware of the fatalities of life—my God, I've good reason to be! Sudden death comes to the strongest man—especially in these days of road casualties. But I'd provided for that. I made a new will about ten days ago."

"Yes?" Superintendent Harper leaned forward.

"I left the sum of fifty thousand pounds to be held in trust for Ruby Keene until she was twenty-five, when she would come into the principal."

Superintendent Harper's eyes opened. So did Colonel Melchett's. Harper said in an almost awed voice:

"That's a very large sum of money, Mr. Jefferson."

"In these days, yes, it is."

"And you were leaving it to a girl you had only known a few weeks?"

Anger flashed into the vivid blue eyes.

"Must I go on repeating the same thing over and over again? I've no flesh and blood of my own—no nieces or nephews or distant cousins, even! I might have left it to charity. I prefer to leave it to an individual." He laughed. "Cinderella turned into a princess overnight! A fairy-godfather instead of a fairy-godmother. Why not? It's *my* money. *I* made it."

Colonel Melchett asked: "Any other bequests?"

"A small legacy to Edwards, my valet—and the remainder to Mark and Addie in equal shares."

"Would—excuse me—the residue amount to a large sum?"

"Probably not. It's difficult to say exactly, investments fluctuate all the time. The sum involved, after death duties and expenses had been paid, would probably have come to something between five and ten thousand pounds net."

"I see."

"And you needn't think I was treating them shabbily. As I said, I divided up my estate at the time my children married. I left myself, actually, a very small sum. But after—after the tragedy—I wanted something to occupy my mind. I flung myself into business. At my house in London I had a private line put in connecting my bedroom with my office. I worked hard—it helped me not to think, and it made me feel that my—my mutilation had not vanquished me. I threw myself into work"—his voice took on a deeper note, he spoke more to himself than to his audience—"and, by some subtle irony, everything I did prospered! My wildest speculations succeeded. If I gambled, I won. Everything I touched turned to gold. Fate's ironic way of righting the balance, I suppose."

The lines of suffering stood out on his face again.

Recollecting himself, he smiled wryly at them.

"So you see, the sum of money I left Ruby was indisputably mine to do with as my fancy dictated."

Melchett said quickly:

"Undoubtedly, my dear fellow, we are not questioning that for a moment."

Conway Jefferson said: "Good. Now I want to ask some questions in my turn, if I may. I want to hear—more about this terrible business. All I know is that she—that little Ruby was found strangled in a house some twenty miles from here."

"That is correct. At Gossington Hall."

Jefferson frowned.

"Gossington? But that's—"

"Colonel Bantry's house."

"Bantry! *Arthur Bantry?* But I know him. Know him and his wife! Met them abroad some years ago. I didn't realize they lived in this part of the world. Why, it's—"

He broke off. Superintendent Harper slipped in smoothly:

"Colonel Bantry was dining in the hotel here Tuesday of last week. You didn't see him?"

"Tuesday? Tuesday? No, we were back late. Went over to Harden Head and had dinner on the way back."

Melchett said:

"Ruby Keene never mentioned the Bantrys to you?"

Jefferson shook his head.

"Never. Don't believe she knew them. Sure she didn't. She didn't know anybody but theatrical folk and that sort of thing." He paused and then asked abruptly:

"What's Bantry got to say about it?"

"He can't account for it in the least. He was out at a Conservative meeting last night. The body was discovered this morning. He says he's never seen the girl in his life."

Jefferson nodded. He said:

"It certainly seems fantastic."

Superintendent Harper cleared his throat. He said:

"Have you any idea at all, sir, who can have done this?"

"Good God, I wish I had!" The veins stood out on his forehead. "It's incredible, unimaginable! I'd say it couldn't have happened, if it hadn't happened!"

"There's no friend of hers—from her past life—no man hanging about—or threatening her?"

"I'm sure there isn't. She'd have told me if so. She's never had a regular 'boyfriend.' She told me so herself."

Superintendent Harper thought:

"Yes, I dare say that's what *she* told you! But that's as may be!"

Conway Jefferson went on:

"Josie would know better than anyone if there had been some man hanging about Ruby or pestering her. Can't she help?"

"She says not."

Jefferson said, frowning:

"I can't help feeling it must be the work of some maniac—the brutality of the method—breaking into a country house—the whole thing so unconnected and senseless. There are men of that type, men outwardly sane, but who decoy girls—sometimes children—away and kill them. Sexual crimes really, I suppose."

Harper said:

"Oh, yes, there are such cases, but we've no knowledge of anyone of that kind operating in this neighbourhood."

Jefferson went on:

"I've thought over all the various men I've seen with Ruby. Guests here and outsiders—men she'd danced with. They all seem harmless enough—

the usual type. She had no special friend of any kind."

Superintendent Harper's face remained quite impassive, but unseen by Conway Jefferson there was still a speculative glint in his eye.

It was quite possible, he thought, that Ruby Keene might have had a special friend even though Conway Jefferson did not know about it.

He said nothing, however. The Chief Constable gave him a glance of inquiry and then rose to his feet. He said:

"Thank you, Mr. Jefferson. That's all we need for the present."

Jefferson said:

"You'll keep me informed of your progress?"

"Yes, yes, we'll keep in touch with you."

The two men went out.

Conway Jefferson leaned back in his chair.

His eyelids came down and veiled the fierce blue of his eyes. He looked suddenly a very tired man.

Then, after a minute or two, the lids flickered. He called: "Edwards!"

From the next room the valet appeared promptly. Edwards knew his master as no one else did. Others, even his nearest, knew only his strength. Edwards knew his weakness. He had seen Conway Jefferson tired, discouraged, weary of life, momentarily defeated by infirmity and loneliness.

"Yes, sir?"

Jefferson said:

"Get on to Sir Henry Clithering. He's at Melborne Abbas. Ask him, from me, to get here today if he can, instead of tomorrow. Tell him it's urgent."

Seven

When they were outside Jefferson's door, Superintendent Harper said:

"Well, for what it's worth, we've got a motive, sir."

"H'm," said Melchett. "Fifty thousand pounds, eh?"

"Yes, sir. Murder's been done for a good deal less than that."

"Yes, but—"

Colonel Melchett left the sentence unfinished. Harper, however, understood him.

"You don't think it's likely in this case? Well, I don't either, as far as that goes. But it's got to be gone into all the same."

"Oh, of course."

Harper went on:

"If, as Mr. Jefferson says, Mr. Gaskell and Mrs. Jefferson are already well provided for and in receipt of a comfortable income, well, it's not likely they'd set out to do a brutal murder."

"Quite so. Their financial standing will have to be investigated, of course. Can't say I like the appearance of Gaskell much—looks a sharp, unscrupulous sort of fellow—but that's a long way from making him out a murderer."

"Oh, yes, sir, as I say, I don't think it's *likely* to be either of them, and from what Josie said I don't see how it would have been humanly possible. They were both playing bridge from twenty minutes to eleven until midnight. No, to my mind there's another possibility much more likely."

Melchett said: "Boy friend of Ruby Keene's?"

"That's it, sir. Some disgruntled young fellow—not too strong in the head, perhaps. Someone, I'd say, she knew before she came here. This adoption scheme, if he got wise to it, may just have put the lid on things. He saw himself losing her, saw her being removed to a different sphere of life altogether, and he went mad and blind with rage. He got her to come out and meet him last night, had a row with her over it, lost his head completely and did her in."

"And how did she come to be in Bantry's library?"

"I think that's feasible. They were out, say, in his car at the time. He came to himself, realized what he'd done, and his first thought was how to get rid of the body. Say they were near the gates of a big house at the time. The idea comes to him that if she's found there the hue and cry will centre round the house and its occupants and will leave him comfortably out of it. She's a little bit of a thing. He could easily carry her. He's got a chisel in the car. He forces a window and plops her down on the hearthrug. Being a strangling case, there's no blood or mess to give him away in the car. See what I mean, sir?"

"Oh, yes, Harper, it's all perfectly possible. But there's still one thing to be done. *Cherchez l'homme.*"

"What? Oh, very good, sir."

Superintendent Harper tactfully applauded his superior's joke, although, owing to the excellence of Colonel Melchett's French accent he almost missed the sense of the words.

II

"Oh—er—I say—er—c-could I speak to you a minute?" It was George Bartlett who thus waylaid the two men. Colonel Melchett, who was not attracted to Mr. Bartlett and who was anxious to see how Slack had got on with the investigation of the girl's room and the questioning of the chambermaids, barked sharply:

"Well, what is it—what is it?"

Young Mr. Bartlett retreated a step or two, opening and shutting his mouth and giving an unconscious imitation of a fish in a tank.

"Well—er—probably isn't important, don't you know—thought I ought to tell you. Matter of fact, can't find my car."

"What do you mean, can't find your car?"

Stammering a good deal, Mr. Bartlett explained that what he meant was that he couldn't find his car.

Superintendent Harper said:

"Do you mean it's been stolen?"

George Bartlett turned gratefully to the more placid voice.

"Well, that's just it, you know. I mean, one can't tell, can one? I mean someone may just have buzzed off in it, not meaning any harm, if you know what I mean."

"When did you last see it, Mr. Bartlett?"

"Well, I was tryin' to remember. Funny how difficult it is to remember anything, isn't it?"

Colonel Melchett said coldly:

"Not, I should think, to a normal intelligence. I understood you to say just now that it was in the courtyard of the hotel last night—"

Mr. Bartlett was bold enough to interrupt. He said:

"That's just it—was it?"

"What do you mean by 'was it'? You said it *was*."

"Well—I mean I *thought* it was. I mean—well, I didn't go out and look, don't you see?"

Colonel Melchett sighed. He summoned all his patience. He said:

"Let's get this quite clear. When was the last time you saw—actually *saw* your car? What make is it, by the way?"

"Minoan 14."

"And you last saw it—when?"

George Bartlett's Adam's apple jerked convulsively up and down.

"Been trying to think. Had it before lunch yesterday. Was going for a spin in the afternoon. But somehow, you know how it is, went to sleep instead. Then, after tea, had a game of squash and all that, and a bathe afterwards."

"And the car was then in the courtyard of the hotel?"

"Suppose so. I mean, that's where I'd put it. Thought, you see, I'd take someone for a spin. After dinner, I mean. But it wasn't my lucky evening. Nothing doing. Never took the old bus out after all."

Harper said:

"But, as far as you knew, the car was still in the courtyard?"

"Well, naturally. I mean, I'd put it there—what?"

"Would you have noticed if it had *not* been there?"

Mr. Bartlett shook his head.

"Don't think so, you know. Lots of cars going and coming and all that. Plenty of Minoans."

Superintendent Harper nodded. He had just cast a casual glance out of the window. There were at that moment no less than eight Minoan 14s in the courtyard—it was the popular cheap car of the year.

"Aren't you in the habit of putting your car away at night?" asked Colonel Melchett.

"Don't usually bother," said Mr. Bartlett. "Fine

weather and all that, you know. Such a fag putting a car away in a garage."

Glancing at Colonel Melchett, Superintendent Harper said: "I'll join you upstairs, sir. I'll just get hold of Sergeant Higgins and he can take down particulars from Mr. Bartlett."

"Right, Harper."

Mr. Bartlett murmured wistfully:

"Thought I ought to let you know, you know. Might be important, what?"

III

Mr. Prestcott had supplied his additional dancer with board and lodging. Whatever the board, the lodging was the poorest the hotel possessed.

Josephine Turner and Ruby Keene had occupied rooms at the extreme end of a mean and dingy little corridor. The rooms were small, faced north on to a portion of the cliff that backed the hotel, and were furnished with the odds and ends of suites that had once, some thirty years ago, represented luxury and magnificence in the best suites. Now, when the hotel had been modernized and the bedrooms supplied with built-in receptacles for clothes, these large Victorian oak and mahogany wardrobes were relegated to those rooms occupied by the hotel's resident staff, or given to guests in the height of the season when all the rest of the hotel was full.

As Melchett saw at once, the position of Ruby Keene's room was ideal for the purpose of leaving the hotel without being observed, and was particularly unfortunate from the point of view of throwing light on the circumstances of that departure.

At the end of the corridor was a small staircase which led down to an equally obscure corridor on the ground floor. Here there was a glass door which led out on to the side terrace of the hotel, an unfrequented terrace with no view. You could go from it to the main terrace in front, or you could go down a winding path and come out in a lane that eventually rejoined the cliff road farther along. Its surface being bad, it was seldom used.

Inspector Slack had been busy harrying chambermaids and examining Ruby's room for clues. He had been lucky enough to find the room exactly as it had been left the night before.

Ruby Keene had not been in the habit of rising early. Her usual procedure, Slack discovered, was to sleep until about ten or half-past and then ring for breakfast. Consequently, since Conway Jefferson had begun his representations to the manager very early, the police had taken charge of things before the chambermaids had touched the room. They had actually not been down that corridor at all. The other rooms there, at this season of the year, were only opened and dusted once a week.

"That's all to the good as far as it goes," Slack explained gloomily. "It means that if there *were* anything to find we'd find it, but there isn't anything."

The Glenshire police had already been over the room for fingerprints, but there were none unaccounted for. Ruby's own, Josie's, and the two chambermaids—one on the morning and one on the evening shift. There were also a couple of prints made by Raymond Starr, but these were accounted for by his story that he had come up with Josie to look for Ruby when she did not appear for the midnight exhibition dance.

There had been a heap of letters and general rubbish in the pigeonholes of the massive mahogany desk in the corner. Slack had just been carefully sorting through them. But he had found nothing of a suggestive nature. Bills, receipts, theatre programmes, cinema stubs, newspaper cuttings, beauty hints torn from magazines. Of the letters there were some from "Lil," apparently a friend from the Palais de Danse, recounting various affairs and gossip, saying they "missed Rube a lot. Mr. Findeison asked after you ever so often! Quite put out, he is! Young Reg has taken up with May now you've gone. Barny asks after you now and then. Things going much as usual. Old Grouser still as mean as ever with us girls. He ticked off Ada for going about with a fellow."

Slack had carefully noted all the names

mentioned. Inquiries would be made—and it was possible some useful information might come to light. To this Colonel Melchett agreed; so did Superintendent Harper, who had joined them. Otherwise the room had little to yield in the way of information.

Across a chair in the middle of the room was the foamy pink dance frock Ruby had worn early in the evening with a pair of pink satin high-heeled shoes kicked off carelessly on the floor. Two sheer silk stockings were rolled into a ball and flung down. One had a ladder in it. Melchett recalled that the dead girl had had bare feet and legs. This, Slack learned, was her custom. She used makeup on her legs instead of stockings and only sometimes wore stockings for dancing, by this means saving expense. The wardrobe door was open and showed a variety of rather flashy evening dresses and a row of shoes below. There was some soiled underwear in the clothes-basket, some nail parings, soiled face-cleaning tissue and bits of cotton wool stained with rouge and nail-polish in the wastepaper basket—in fact, nothing out of the ordinary! The facts seemed plain to read. Ruby Keene had hurried upstairs, changed her clothes and hurried off again—*where?*

Josephine Turner, who might be supposed to know most of Ruby's life and friends, had proved unable to help. But this, as Inspector Slack pointed out, might be natural.

"If what you tell me is true, sir—about this adoption business, I mean—well, Josie would be all for Ruby breaking with any old friends she might have and who might queer the pitch, so to speak. As I see it, this invalid gentleman gets all worked up about Ruby Keene being such a sweet, innocent, childish little piece of goods. Now, supposing Ruby's got a tough boy friend—that won't go down so well with the old boy. So it's Ruby's business to keep that dark. Josie doesn't know much about the girl anyway—not about her friends and all that. But one thing she wouldn't stand for—Ruby's messing up things by carrying on with some undesirable fellow. So it stands to reason that Ruby (who, as I see it, was a sly little piece!) would keep very dark about seeing any old friend. She wouldn't let on to Josie anything about it—otherwise Josie would say: 'No, you don't, my girl.' But you know what girls are—especially young ones—always ready to make a fool of themselves over a tough guy. Ruby wants to see him. He comes down here, cuts up rough about the whole business, and wrings the girl's neck."

"I expect you're right, Slack," said Colonel Melchett, disguising his usual repugnance for the unpleasant way Slack had of putting things. "If so, we ought to be able to discover this tough friend's identity fairly easily."

"You leave it to me, sir," said Slack with his

usual confidence. "I'll get hold of this 'Lil' girl at that Palais de Danse place and turn her right inside out. We'll soon get at the truth."

Colonel Melchett wondered if they would. Slack's energy and activity always made him feel tired.

"There's one other person you might be able to get a tip from, sir," went on Slack, "and that's the dance and tennis pro fellow. He must have seen a lot of her and he'd know more than Josie would. Likely enough she'd loosen her tongue a bit to him."

"I have already discussed that point with Superintendent Harper."

"Good, sir. *I've* done the chambermaids pretty thoroughly! They don't know a thing. Looked down on these two, as far as I can make out. Scamped the service as much as they dared. Chambermaid was in here last at seven o'clock last night, when she turned down the bed and drew the curtains and cleared up a bit. There's a bathroom next door, if you'd like to see it?"

The bathroom was situated between Ruby's room and the slightly larger room occupied by Josie. It was illuminating. Colonel Melchett silently marvelled at the amount of aids to beauty that women could use. Rows of jars of face cream, cleansing cream, vanishing cream, skin-feeding cream! Boxes of different shades of powder. An untidy heap of every variety of lipstick. Hair lotions and "brightening" applications. Eyelash black, mascara, blue stain for under the eyes, at least twelve different shades of nail varnish, face tissues, bits of cotton wool, dirty powder-puffs. Bottles of lotions—astringent, tonic, soothing, etc.

"Do you mean to say," he murmured feebly, "that women use all these things?"

Inspector Slack, who always knew everything, kindly enlightened him.

"In private life, sir, so to speak, a lady keeps to one or two distinct shades, one for evening, one for day. They know what suits them and they keep to it. But these professional girls, they have to ring a change, so to speak. They do exhibition dances, and one night it's a tango and the next a crinoline Victorian dance and then a kind of Apache dance and then just ordinary ballroom, and, of course, the makeup varies a good bit."

"Good lord!" said the Colonel. "No wonder the people who turn out these creams and messes make a fortune."

"Easy money, that's what it is," said Slack. "Easy money. Got to spend a bit in advertisement, of course."

Colonel Melchett jerked his mind away from the fascinating and age-long problem of woman's adornments. He said to Harper, who had just joined them:

"There's still this dancing fellow. Your pigeon, Superintendent?"

"I suppose so, sir."

As they went downstairs Harper asked:

"What did you think of Mr. Bartlett's story, sir?"

"About his car? I think, Harper, that that young man wants watching. It's a fishy story. Supposing that he did take Ruby Keene out in that car last night, after all?"

IV

Superintendent Harper's manner was slow and pleasant and absolutely noncommittal. These cases where the police of two counties had to collaborate were always difficult. He liked Colonel Melchett and considered him an able Chief Constable, but he was nevertheless glad to be tackling the present interview by himself. Never do too much at once, was Superintendent Harper's rule. Bare routine inquiry for the first time. That left the persons you were interviewing relieved and predisposed them to be more unguarded in the next interview you had with them.

Harper already knew Raymond Starr by sight. A fine-looking specimen, tall, lithe, and good-looking, with very white teeth in a deeply-bronzed face. He was dark and graceful. He had a pleasant, friendly manner and was very popular in the hotel.

"I'm afraid I can't help you much, Superintendent. I knew Ruby quite well, of course. She'd been here over a month and we had practised our dances together and all that. But there's really very little to say. She was quite a pleasant and rather stupid girl."

"It's her friendships we're particularly anxious to know about. Her friendships with men."

"So I suppose. Well, *I* don't know anything! She'd got a few young men in tow in the hotel, but nothing special. You see, she was nearly always monopolized by the Jefferson family."

"Yes, the Jefferson family." Harper paused meditatively. He shot a shrewd glance at the young man. "What did you think of that business, Mr. Starr?"

Raymond Starr said coolly: "What business?"

Harper said: "Did you know that Mr. Jefferson was proposing to adopt Ruby Keene legally?"

This appeared to be news to Starr. He pursed up his lips and whistled. He said:

"The clever little devil! Oh, well, there's no fool like an old fool."

"That's how it strikes you, is it?"

"Well—what else can one say? If the old boy wanted to adopt someone, why didn't he pick upon a girl of his own class?"

"Ruby Keene never mentioned the matter to you?"

"No, she didn't. I knew she was elated about something, but I didn't know what it was."

"And Josie?"

"Oh, I think Josie must have known what was in the wind. Probably she was the one who planned the whole thing. Josie's no fool. She's got a head on her, that girl."

Harper nodded. It was Josie who had sent for Ruby Keene. Josie, no doubt, who had encouraged the intimacy. No wonder she had been upset when Ruby had failed to show up for her dance that night and Conway Jefferson had begun to panic. She was envisaging her plans going awry.

He asked:

"Could Ruby keep a secret, do you think?"

"As well as most. She didn't talk about her own affairs much."

"Did she ever say anything—anything at all— about some friend of hers—someone from her former life who was coming to see her here, or whom she had had difficulty with—you know the sort of thing I mean, no doubt."

"I know perfectly. Well, as far as I'm aware, there was no one of the kind. Not by anything she ever said."

"Thank you, Mr. Starr. Now will you just tell me in your own words exactly what happened last night?"

"Certainly. Ruby and I did our ten-thirty dance together—"

"No signs of anything unusual about her then?" Raymond considered.

"I don't think so. I didn't notice what happened afterwards. I had my own partners to look after. I do remember noticing she wasn't in the ballroom. At midnight she hadn't turned up. I was very annoyed and went to Josie about it. Josie was playing bridge with the Jeffersons. She hadn't any idea where Ruby was, and I think she got a bit of a jolt. I noticed her shoot a quick, anxious glance at Mr. Jefferson. I persuaded the band to play another dance and I went to the office and got them to ring up to Ruby's room. There wasn't any answer. I went back to Josie. She suggested that Ruby was perhaps asleep in her room. Idiotic suggestion really, but it was meant for the Jeffersons, of course! She came away with me and said we'd go up together."

"Yes, Mr. Starr. And what did she say when she was alone with you?"

"As far as I can remember, she looked very angry and said: 'Damned little fool. She can't do this sort of thing. It will ruin all her chances. Who's she with, do you know?'

"I said that I hadn't the least idea. The last I'd seen of her was dancing with young Bartlett. Josie said: 'She wouldn't be with *him*. What *can* she be up to? She isn't with that film man, is she?'"

Harper said sharply: "*Film man?* Who was he?"

Raymond said: "I don't know his name. He's never stayed here. Rather an unusual-looking chap—black hair and theatrical-looking. He has something to do with the film industry, I believe—or so he told Ruby. He came over to dine here once or twice and danced with Ruby afterwards, but I don't think she knew him at all well. That's why I was surprised when Josie mentioned him. I said I didn't think he'd been here tonight. Josie said: 'Well, she must be out with *someone*. What on earth am I going to say to the Jeffersons?' I said what did it matter to the Jeffersons? And Josie said it *did* matter. And she said, too, that she'd never forgive Ruby if she went and messed things up.

"We'd got to Ruby's room by then. She wasn't there, of course, but she'd been there, because the dress she had been wearing was lying across a chair. Josie looked in the wardrobe and said she thought she'd put on her old white dress. Normally she'd have changed into a black velvet dress for our Spanish dance. I was pretty angry by this time at the way Ruby had let me down. Josie did her best to soothe me and said she'd dance herself so that old Prestcott shouldn't get after us all. She went away and changed her dress and we went down and did a tango—exaggerated style and quite showy but not really too exhausting upon the ankles. Josie was very plucky about it—

for it hurt her, I could see. After that she asked me to help her soothe the Jeffersons down. She said it was important. So, of course, I did what I could."

Superintendent Harper nodded. He said:

"Thank you, Mr. Starr."

To himself he thought: "It was important, all right! Fifty thousand pounds!"

He watched Raymond Starr as the latter moved gracefully away. He went down the steps of the terrace, picking up a bag of tennis balls and a racquet on the way. Mrs. Jefferson, also carrying a racquet, joined him and they went towards the tennis courts.

"Excuse me, sir."

Sergeant Higgins, rather breathless, stood at Harper's side.

The Superintendent, jerked from the train of thought he was following, looked startled.

"Message just come through for you from headquarters, sir. Labourer reported this morning saw glare as of fire. Half an hour ago they found a burnt-out car in a quarry. Venn's Quarry—about two miles from here. Traces of a charred body inside."

A flush came over Harper's heavy features. He said:

"What's come to Glenshire? An epidemic of violence? Don't tell me we're going to have a Rouse case now!"

He asked: "Could they get the number of the car?"

"No, sir. But we'll be able to identify it, of course, by the engine number. A Minoan 14, they think it is."

Eight

Sir Henry Clithering, as he passed through the lounge of the Majestic, hardly glanced at its occupants. His mind was preoccupied. Nevertheless, as is the way of life, something registered in his subconscious. It waited its time patiently.

Sir Henry was wondering as he went upstairs just what had induced the sudden urgency of his friend's message. Conway Jefferson was not the type of man who sent urgent summonses to anyone. Something quite out of the usual must have occurred, decided Sir Henry.

Jefferson wasted no time in beating about the bush. He said:

"Glad you've come. Edwards, get Sir Henry a drink. Sit down, man. You've not heard anything, I suppose? Nothing in the papers yet?"

Sir Henry shook his head, his curiosity aroused.

"What's the matter?"

"Murder's the matter. I'm concerned in it and so are your friends the Bantrys."

"Arthur and Dolly Bantry?" Clithering sounded incredulous.

"Yes, you see, the body was found in their house."

Clearly and succinctly, Conway Jefferson ran through the facts. Sir Henry listened without interrupting. Both men were accustomed to grasping the gist of a matter. Sir Henry, during his term as Commissioner of the Metropolitan Police, had been renowned for his quick grip on essentials.

"It's an extraordinary business," he commented when the other had finished. "How do the Bantrys come into it, do you think?"

"That's what worries me. You see, Henry, it looks to me as though possibly the fact that I know them might have a bearing on the case. That's the only connection I can find. Neither of them, I gather, ever saw the girl before. That's what they say, and there's no reason to disbelieve them. It's most unlikely they *should* know her. Then isn't it possible that she was decoyed away and her body deliberately left in the house of friends of mine?"

Clithering said:

"I think that's far-fetched."

"It's possible, though," persisted the other.

"Yes, but unlikely. What do you want *me* to do?"

Conway Jefferson said bitterly:

"I'm an invalid. I disguise the fact—refuse to face it—but now it comes home to me. I can't go about as I'd like to, asking questions, looking into things. I've got to stay here meekly grateful for such scraps of information as the police are kind enough to dole out to me. Do you happen to know

Melchett, by the way, the Chief Constable of Radfordshire?"

"Yes, I've met him."

Something stirred in Sir Henry's brain. A face and figure noted unseeingly as he passed through the lounge. A straight-backed old lady whose face was familiar. It linked up with the last time he had seen Melchett.

He said:

"Do you mean you want me to be a kind of amateur sleuth? That's not my line."

Jefferson said:

"You're *not* an amateur, that's just it."

"I'm not a professional anymore. I'm on the retired list now."

Jefferson said: "That simplifies matters."

"You mean that if I were still at Scotland Yard I couldn't butt in? That's perfectly true."

"As it is," said Jefferson, "your experience qualifies you to take an interest in the case, and any cooperation you offer will be welcomed."

Clithering said slowly:

"Etiquette permits, I agree. But what do you really want, Conway? To find out who killed this girl?"

"Just that."

"You've no idea yourself?"

"None whatever."

Sir Henry said slowly:

"You probably won't believe me, but you've

got an expert at solving mysteries sitting downstairs in the lounge at this minute. Someone who's better than I am at it, and who in all probability *may* have some local dope."

"What are you talking about?"

"Downstairs in the lounge, by the third pillar from the left, there sits an old lady with a sweet, placid spinsterish face, and a mind that has plumbed the depths of human iniquity and taken it as all in the day's work. Her name's Miss Marple. She comes from the village of St. Mary Mead, which is a mile and a half from Gossington, she's a friend of the Bantrys—and where crime is concerned she's the goods, Conway."

Jefferson stared at him with thick, puckered brows. He said heavily:

"You're joking."

"No, I'm not. You spoke of Melchett just now. The last time I saw Melchett there was a village tragedy. Girl supposed to have drowned herself. Police quite rightly suspected that it wasn't suicide, but murder. They thought they knew who did it. Along to me comes old Miss Marple, fluttering and dithering. She's afraid, she says, they'll hang the wrong person. She's got no evidence, but she knows who did do it. Hands me a piece of paper with a name written on it. And, by God, Jefferson, she was right!"

Conway Jefferson's brows came down lower than ever. He grunted disbelievingly:

"Woman's intuition, I suppose," he said sceptically.

"No, she doesn't call it that. Specialized knowledge is her claim."

"And what does that mean?"

"Well, you know, Jefferson, *we* use it in police work. We get a burglary and we usually know pretty well who did it—of the regular crowd, that is. We know the sort of burglar who acts in a particular sort of way. Miss Marple has an interesting, though occasionally trivial, series of parallels from village life."

Jefferson said sceptically:

"What is she likely to know about a girl who's been brought up in a theatrical milieu and probably never been in a village in her life?"

"I think," said Sir Henry Clithering firmly, "that she might have ideas."

II

Miss Marple flushed with pleasure as Sir Henry bore down upon her.

"Oh, Sir Henry, this is indeed a great piece of luck meeting you here."

Sir Henry was gallant. He said:

"To me it is a great pleasure."

Miss Marple murmured, flushing: "So kind of you."

"Are you staying here?"

"Well, as a matter of fact, we are."

"*We?*"

"Mrs. Bantry's here too." She looked at him sharply. "Have you heard yet? Yes, I can see you have. It is terrible, is it not?"

"What's Dolly Bantry doing here? Is her husband here too?"

"No. Naturally, they both reacted quite differently. Colonel Bantry, poor man, just shuts himself up in his study, or goes down to one of the farms, when anything like this happens. Like tortoises, you know, they draw their heads in and hope nobody will notice them. Dolly, of course, is *quite* different."

"Dolly, in fact," said Sir Henry, who knew his old friend fairly well, "is almost enjoying herself, eh?"

"Well—er—yes. Poor dear."

"And she's brought you along to produce the rabbits out of the hat for her?"

Miss Marple said composedly:

"Dolly thought that a change of scene would be a good thing and she didn't want to come alone." She met his eye and her own gently twinkled. "But, of course, your way of describing it is quite true. It's rather embarrassing for me, because, of course, I am no use at all."

"No ideas? No village parallels?"

"I don't know very much about it all yet."

"I can remedy that, I think. I'm going to call you into consultation, Miss Marple."

He gave a brief recital of the course of events. Miss Marple listened with keen interest.

"Poor Mr. Jefferson," she said. "What a very sad story. These terrible accidents. To leave him alive, crippled, seems more cruel than if he had been killed too."

"Yes, indeed. That's why all his friends admire him so much for the resolute way he's gone on, conquering pain and grief and physical disabilities."

"Yes, it is splendid."

"The only thing I can't understand is this sudden outpouring of affection for this girl. She may, of course, have had some remarkable qualities."

"Probably not," said Miss Marple placidly.

"You don't think so?"

"I don't think her qualities entered into it."

Sir Henry said:

"He isn't just a nasty old man, you know."

"Oh, no, no!" Miss Marple got quite pink. "I wasn't implying that for a minute. What I was trying to say was—very badly, I know—that he was just looking for a nice bright girl to take his dead daughter's place—and then this girl saw her opportunity and played it for all she was worth! That sounds rather uncharitable, I know, but I have seen so many cases of the kind. The young maid-servant at Mr. Harbottle's, for instance. A *very* ordinary girl, but quiet with nice manners.

122

His sister was called away to nurse a dying relative and when she got back she found the girl completely above herself, sitting down in the drawing room laughing and talking and not wearing her cap or apron. Miss Harbottle spoke to her very sharply and the girl was impertinent, and then old Mr. Harbottle left her quite dumbfounded by saying that he thought she had kept house for him long enough and that he was making other arrangements.

"Such a scandal as it created in the village, but poor Miss Harbottle had to go and live *most* uncomfortably in rooms in Eastbourne. People *said* things, of course, but I believe there was no familiarity of any kind—it was simply that the old man found it much pleasanter to have a young, cheerful girl telling him how clever and amusing he was than to have his sister continually pointing out his faults to him, even if she *was* a good economical manager."

There was a moment's pause, and then Miss Marple resumed.

"And there was Mr. Badger who had the chemist's shop. Made a lot of fuss over the young lady who worked in his toilet section. Told his wife they must look on her as a daughter and have her to live in the house. Mrs. Badger didn't see it that way at all."

Sir Henry said: "If she'd only been a girl in his own rank of life—a friend's child—"

Miss Marple interrupted him.

"Oh! but that wouldn't have been nearly as satisfactory from his point of view. It's like King Cophetua and the beggar maid. If you're really rather a lonely, tired old man, and if, perhaps, your own family have been neglecting you"—she paused for a second—"well, to befriend someone who will be overwhelmed with your magnificence—(to put it rather melodramatically, but I hope you see what I mean)—well, that's much more interesting. It makes you feel a much greater person—a beneficent monarch! The recipient is more likely to be dazzled, and that, of course, is a pleasant feeling for you." She paused and said: "Mr. Badger, you know, bought the girl in his shop some really fantastic presents, a diamond bracelet and a most expensive radio-gramophone. Took out a lot of his savings to do so. However, Mrs. Badger, who was a much more astute woman than poor Miss Harbottle (marriage, of course, *helps*), took the trouble to find out a few things. And when Mr. Badger discovered that the girl was carrying on with a *very* undesirable young man connected with the racecourses, and had actually pawned the bracelet to give him the money—well, he was completely disgusted and the affair passed over quite safely. And he gave Mrs. Badger a diamond ring the following Christmas."

Her pleasant, shrewd eyes met Sir Henry's. He

wondered if what she had been saying was intended as a hint. He said:

"Are you suggesting that if there had been a young man in Ruby Keene's life, my friend's attitude towards her might have altered?"

"It probably would, you know. I dare say, in a year or two, he might have liked to arrange for her marriage himself—though more likely he wouldn't—gentlemen are usually rather selfish. But I certainly think that if Ruby Keene had had a young man she'd have been careful to keep very quiet about it."

"And the young man might have resented that?"

"I suppose that *is* the most plausible solution. It struck me, you know, that her cousin, the young woman who was at Gossington this morning, looked definitely *angry* with the dead girl. What you've told me explains *why*. No doubt she was looking forward to doing very well out of the business."

"Rather a cold-blooded character, in fact?"

"That's too harsh a judgment, perhaps. The poor thing has had to earn her living, and you can't expect her to sentimentalize because a well-to-do man and woman—as you have described Mr. Gaskell and Mrs. Jefferson—are going to be done out of a further large sum of money to which they have really no particular moral right. I should say Miss Turner was a hard-headed, ambitious young woman, with a good temper and considerable *joie de vivre*. A little," added Miss Marple, "like Jessie Golden, the baker's daughter."

"What happened to her?" asked Sir Henry.

"She trained as a nursery governess and married the son of the house, who was home on leave from India. Made him a very good wife, I believe."

Sir Henry pulled himself clear of these fascinating side issues. He said:

"Is there any reason, do you think, why my friend Conway Jefferson should suddenly have developed this 'Cophetua complex,' if you like to call it that?"

"There might have been."

"In what way?"

Miss Marple said, hesitating a little:

"I should think—it's only a suggestion, of course—that perhaps his son-in-law and daughter-in-law *might* have wanted to get married again."

"Surely he couldn't have objected to that?"

"Oh, no, not *objected*. But, you see, you must look at it from *his* point of view. He had a terrible shock and loss—so had they. The three bereaved people live together and the *link* between them is the loss they have all sustained. But Time, as my dear mother used to say, is a great healer. Mr. Gaskell and Mrs. Jefferson are young. Without knowing it themselves, they may have begun to feel restless, to resent the bonds that tied them to their past sorrow. And so, feeling like that, old Mr. Jefferson would have become conscious of a sudden lack of sympathy without knowing its cause. It's usually that. Gentlemen so *easily* feel neglected. With Mr. Harbottle it was Miss Harbottle going away. And with the Badgers it was Mrs. Badger taking such an interest in Spiritualism and always going out to séances."

"I must say," said Sir Henry ruefully, "that I dislike the way you reduce us all to a General Common Denominator."

Miss Marple shook her head sadly.

"Human nature is very much the same anywhere, Sir Henry."

Sir Henry said distastefully:

"Mr. Harbottle! Mr. Badger! And poor Conway! I hate to intrude the personal note, but have you any parallel for *my* humble self in your village?"

"Well, of course, there is Briggs."

"Who's Briggs?"

"He was the head gardener up at Old Hall. *Quite* the best man they ever had. Knew *exactly* when the under-gardeners were slacking off— quite uncanny it was! He managed with only three men and a boy and the place was kept better than it had been with six. And took several firsts with his sweet peas. He's retired now."

"Like me," said Sir Henry.

"But he still does a little jobbing—if he likes the people."

"Ah," said Sir Henry. "Again like me. That's what I'm doing now—jobbing—to help an old friend."

"Two old friends."

"Two?" Sir Henry looked a little puzzled.

Miss Marple said:

"I suppose you meant Mr. Jefferson. But I wasn't thinking of him. I was thinking of Colonel and Mrs. Bantry."

"Yes—yes—I see—" He asked sharply: "Was that why you alluded to Dolly Bantry as 'poor dear' at the beginning of our conversation?"

"Yes. She hasn't begun to realize things yet. *I* know because I've had more experience. You see, Sir Henry, it seems to me that there's a great possibility of this crime being the kind of crime that never *does* get solved. Like the Brighton trunk murders. But if that happens it will be absolutely disastrous for the Bantrys. Colonel Bantry, like nearly all retired military men, is really *abnormally* sensitive. He reacts very quickly to public opinion. He won't notice it for some time, and then it will begin to go home to him. A slight here, and a snub there, and invitations that are refused, and excuses that are made—and then, little by little, it will dawn upon him and he'll retire into his shell and get terribly morbid and miserable."

"Let me be sure I understand you rightly, Miss

Marple. You mean that, because the body was found in his house, people will think that *he* had something to do with it?"

"Of course they will! I've no doubt they're saying so already. They'll say so more and more. And people will cold shoulder the Bantrys and avoid them. That's why the truth has got to be found out and why I was willing to come here with Mrs. Bantry. An open accusation is one thing—and quite easy for a soldier to meet. He's indignant and he has a chance of fighting. But this other *whispering* business will break him— will break them both. So you see, Sir Henry, we've *got* to find out the truth."

Sir Henry said:

"Any ideas as to why the body should have been found in his house? There must be an explanation of that. Some connection."

"Oh, of course."

"The girl was last seen here about twenty minutes to eleven. By midnight, according to the medical evidence, she was dead. Gossington's about eighteen miles from here. Good road for sixteen of those miles until one turns off the main road. A powerful car could do it in well under half an hour. Practically *any* car could average thirty-five. But why anyone should either kill her here and take her body out to Gossington or should take her out to Gossington and strangle her there, I don't know."

"Of course you don't, because it didn't happen."

"Do you mean that she was strangled by some fellow who took her out in a car and he then decided to push her into the first likely house in the neighbourhood?"

"I don't think anything of the kind. I think there was a very careful plan made. What happened was that the plan went wrong."

Sir Henry stared at her.

"Why did the plan go wrong?"

Miss Marple said rather apologetically:

"Such curious things happen, don't they? If I were to say that this particular plan went wrong because human beings are so much more vulnerable and sensitive than anyone thinks, it wouldn't sound sensible, would it? But that's what I believe—and—"

She broke off. "Here's Mrs. Bantry now."

Nine

Mrs. Bantry was with Adelaide Jefferson. The former came up to Sir Henry and exclaimed: *"You?"*

"I, myself." He took both her hands and pressed them warmly. "I can't tell you how distressed I am at all this, Mrs. B."

Mrs. Bantry said mechanically:

"Don't call me Mrs. B.!" and went on: "Arthur isn't here. He's taking it all rather seriously. Miss Marple and I have come here to sleuth. Do you know Mrs. Jefferson?"

"Yes, of course."

He shook hands. Adelaide Jefferson said:

"Have you seen my father-in-law?"

"Yes, I have."

"I'm glad. We're anxious about him. It was a terrible shock."

Mrs. Bantry said:

"Let's come out on the terrace and have drinks and talk about it all."

The four of them went out and joined Mark Gaskell, who was sitting at the extreme end of the terrace by himself.

After a few desultory remarks and the arrival of the drinks Mrs. Bantry plunged straight into the subject with her usual zest for direct action.

"We can talk about it, can't we?" she said. "I

131

mean, we're all old friends—except Miss Marple, and she knows all about crime. And she wants to help."

Mark Gaskell looked at Miss Marple in a somewhat puzzled fashion. He said doubtfully:

"Do you—er—write detective stories?"

The most unlikely people, he knew, wrote detective stories. And Miss Marple, in her old-fashioned spinster's clothes, looked a singularly unlikely person.

"Oh no, I'm not clever enough for *that*."

"She's wonderful," said Mrs. Bantry impatiently. "I can't explain now, but she is. Now, Addie, I want to know all about things. What was she really like, this girl?"

"Well—" Adelaide Jefferson paused, glanced across at Mark, and half laughed. She said: "You're so direct."

"Did you like her?"

"No, of course I didn't."

"What was she really like?" Mrs. Bantry shifted her inquiry to Mark Gaskell. Mark said deliberately:

"Common or garden gold-digger. And she knew her stuff. She'd got her hooks into Jeff all right."

Both of them called their father-in-law Jeff.

Sir Henry thought, looking disapprovingly at Mark:

"Indiscreet fellow. Shouldn't be so outspoken."

He had always disapproved a little of Mark

Gaskell. The man had charm but he was unreliable—talked too much, was occasionally boastful—not quite to be trusted, Sir Henry thought. He had sometimes wondered if Conway Jefferson thought so too.

"But couldn't you *do* something about it?" demanded Mrs. Bantry.

Mark said dryly:

"We might have—if we'd realized it in time."

He shot a glance at Adelaide and she coloured faintly. There had been reproach in that glance.

She said:

"Mark thinks I ought to have seen what was coming."

"You left the old boy alone too much, Addie. Tennis lessons and all the rest of it."

"Well, I had to have some exercise." She spoke apologetically. "Anyway, I never dreamed—"

"No," said Mark, "neither of us ever dreamed. Jeff has always been such a sensible, levelheaded old boy."

Miss Marple made a contribution to the conversation.

"Gentlemen," she said with her old-maid's way of referring to the opposite sex as though it were a species of wild animal, "are frequently not as levelheaded as they seem."

"I'll say you're right," said Mark. "Unfortunately, Miss Marple, we didn't realize that. We wondered what the old boy saw in that rather insipid and meretricious little bag of tricks. But we were pleased for him to be kept happy and amused. We thought there was no harm in her. No harm in her! I wish I'd wrung her neck!"

"Mark," said Addie, "you really *must* be careful what you say."

He grinned at her engagingly.

"I suppose I must. Otherwise people will think I actually *did* wring her neck. Oh well, I suppose I'm under suspicion, anyway. If anyone had an interest in seeing that girl dead it was Addie and myself."

"Mark," cried Mrs. Jefferson, half laughing and half angry, "you really *mustn't!*"

"All right, all right," said Mark Gaskell pacifically. "But I do like speaking my mind. Fifty thousand pounds our esteemed father-in-law was proposing to settle upon that half-baked nitwitted little slypuss."

"Mark, you mustn't—she's dead."

"Yes, she's dead, poor little devil. And after all, why shouldn't she use the weapons that Nature gave her? Who am I to judge? Done plenty of rotten things myself in my life. No, let's say Ruby was entitled to plot and scheme and we were mugs not to have tumbled to her game sooner."

Sir Henry said:

"What did you say when Conway told you he proposed to adopt the girl?"

Mark thrust out his hands.

"What could we say? Addie, always the little lady, retained her self-control admirably. Put a brave face upon it. I endeavoured to follow her example."

"*I* should have made a fuss!" said Mrs. Bantry.

"Well, frankly speaking, we weren't entitled to make a fuss. It was Jeff's money. We weren't his flesh and blood. He'd always been damned good to us. There was nothing for it but to bite on the bullet." He added reflectively: "But we didn't love little Ruby."

Adelaide Jefferson said:

"If only it had been some other kind of girl. Jeff had two godchildren, you know. If it had been one of them—well, one would have *understood* it." She added, with a shade of resentment: "And Jeff's always seemed so fond of Peter."

"Of course," said Mrs. Bantry. "I always have known Peter was your first husband's child—but I'd quite forgotten it. I've always thought of him as Mr. Jefferson's grandson."

"So have I," said Adelaide. Her voice held a note that made Miss Marple turn in her chair and look at her.

"It was Josie's fault," said Mark. "Josie brought her here."

Adelaide said:

"Oh, but surely you don't think it was deliberate, do you? Why, you've always liked Josie so much."

135

"Yes, I did like her. I thought she was a good sport."

"It was sheer accident her bringing the girl down."

"Josie's got a good head on her shoulders, my girl."

"Yes, but she couldn't foresee—"

Mark said:

"No, she couldn't. I admit it. I'm not really accusing her of planning the whole thing. But I've no doubt she saw which way the wind was blowing long before we did and kept very quiet about it."

Adelaide said with a sigh:

"I suppose one can't blame her for that."

Mark said:

"Oh, we can't blame anyone for anything!"

Mrs. Bantry asked:

"Was Ruby Keene very pretty?"

Mark stared at her. "I thought you'd seen—"

Mrs. Bantry said hastily:

"Oh yes, I saw her—her body. But she'd been strangled, you know, and one couldn't tell—" She shivered.

Mark said, thoughtfully:

"I don't think she was really pretty at all. She certainly wouldn't have been without any makeup. A thin ferrety little face, not much chin, teeth running down her throat, nondescript sort of nose—"

"It sounds revolting," said Mrs. Bantry.

"Oh no, she wasn't. As I say, with makeup she managed to give quite an effect of good looks, don't you think so, Addie?"

"Yes, rather chocolate-box, pink and white business. She had nice blue eyes."

"Yes, innocent baby stare, and the heavily-blacked lashes brought out the blueness. Her hair was bleached, of course. It's true, when I come to think of it, that in colouring—artificial colouring, anyway—she had a kind of spurious resemblance to Rosamund—my wife, you know. I dare say that's what attracted the old man's attention to her."

He sighed.

"Well, it's a bad business. The awful thing is that Addie and I can't help being glad, really, that she's dead—"

He quelled a protest from his sister-in-law.

"It's no good, Addie; I know what you feel. I feel the same. And I'm not going to pretend! But, at the same time, if you know what I mean, I really am most awfully concerned for Jeff about the whole business. It's hit him very hard. I—"

He stopped, and stared towards the doors leading out of the lounge on to the terrace.

"Well, well—see who's here. What an unscrupulous woman you are, Addie."

Mrs. Jefferson looked over her shoulder, uttered an exclamation and got up, a slight colour rising in her face. She walked quickly along the terrace and went up to a tall middle-aged man with a thin brown face, who was looking uncertainly about him.

Mrs. Bantry said: "Isn't that Hugo McLean?"

Mark Gaskell said:

"Hugo McLean it is. Alias William Dobbin."

Mrs. Bantry murmured:

"He's very faithful, isn't he?"

"Dog-like devotion," said Mark. "Addie's only got to whistle and Hugo comes trotting from any odd corner of the globe. Always hopes that some day she'll marry him. I dare say she will."

Miss Marple looked beamingly after them. She said:

"I see. A romance?"

"One of the good old-fashioned kind," Mark assured her. "It's been going on for years. Addie's that kind of woman."

He added meditatively: "I suppose Addie telephoned him this morning. She didn't tell me she had."

Edwards came discreetly along the terrace and paused at Mark's elbow.

"Excuse me, sir. Mr. Jefferson would like you to come up."

"I'll come at once." Mark sprang up.

He nodded to them, said: "See you later," and went off.

Sir Henry leant forward to Miss Marple. He said:

"Well, what do you think of the principal beneficiaries of the crime?"

Miss Marple said thoughtfully, looking at Adelaide Jefferson as she stood talking to her old friend:

"I should think, you know, that she was a very devoted mother."

"Oh, she is," said Mrs. Bantry. "She's simply devoted to Peter."

"She's the kind of woman," said Miss Marple, "that everyone likes. The kind of woman that could go on getting married again and again. I don't mean a *man's* woman—that's quite different."

"I know what you mean," said Sir Henry.

"What you both mean," said Mrs. Bantry, "is that she's a good listener."

Sir Henry laughed. He said:

"And Mark Gaskell?"

"Ah," said Miss Marple, "he's a downy fellow."

"Village parallel, please?"

"Mr. Cargill, the builder. He bluffed a lot of people into having things done to their houses they never meant to do. And how he charged them for it! But he could always explain his bills away plausibly. A downy fellow. He married money. So did Mr. Gaskell, I understand."

"You don't like him."

"Yes, I do. Most women would. But he can't take me in. He's a very attractive person, I think.

139

But a little unwise, perhaps, to *talk* as much as he does."

"Unwise is the word," said Sir Henry. "Mark will get himself into trouble if he doesn't look out."

A tall dark young man in white flannels came up the steps to the terrace and paused just for a minute, watching Adelaide Jefferson and Hugo McLean.

"And that," said Sir Henry obligingly, "is X, whom we might describe as an interested party. He is the tennis and dancing pro—Raymond Starr, Ruby Keene's partner."

Miss Marple looked at him with interest. She said:

"He's very nice-looking, isn't he?"

"I suppose so."

"Don't be absurd, Sir Henry," said Mrs. Bantry; "there's no supposing about it. He *is* good-looking."

Miss Marple murmured:

"Mrs. Jefferson has been taking tennis lessons, I think she said."

"Do you mean anything by that, Jane, or don't you?"

Miss Marple had no chance of replying to this downright question. Young Peter Carmody came across the terrace and joined them. He addressed himself to Sir Henry:

"I say, are you a detective, too? I saw you

talking to the Superintendent—the fat one is a superintendent, isn't he?"

"Quite right, my son."

"And somebody told me you were a frightfully important detective from London. The head of Scotland Yard or something like that."

"The head of Scotland Yard is usually a complete dud in books, isn't he?"

"Oh no, not nowadays. Making fun of the police is very old-fashioned. Do you know who did the murder yet?"

"Not yet, I'm afraid."

"Are you enjoying this very much, Peter?" asked Mrs. Bantry.

"Well, I am, rather. It makes a change, doesn't it? I've been hunting round to see if I could find any clues, but I haven't been lucky. I've got a souvenir, though. Would you like to see it? Fancy, Mother wanted me to throw it away. I do think one's parents are rather trying sometimes."

He produced from his pocket a small matchbox. Pushing it open, he disclosed the precious contents.

"See, *it's a fingernail. Her fingernail!* I'm going to label it *Fingernail of the Murdered Woman* and take it back to school. It's a good souvenir, don't you think?"

"Where did you get it?" asked Miss Marple.

"Well, it was a bit of luck, really. Because, of course, I didn't know she was going to be murdered *then*. It was before dinner last night. Ruby caught her nail in Josie's shawl and it tore it. Mums cut it off for her and gave it to me and said put it in the wastepaper basket, and I meant to, but I put it in my pocket instead, and this morning I remembered and looked to see if it was still there and it was, so now I've got it as a souvenir."

"Disgusting," said Mrs. Bantry.

Peter said politely: "Oh, do you think so?"

"Got any other souvenirs?" asked Sir Henry.

"Well, I don't know. I've got something that might be."

"Explain yourself, young man."

Peter looked at him thoughtfully. Then he pulled out an envelope. From the inside of it he extracted a piece of browny tapey substance.

"It's a bit of that chap George Bartlett's shoe-lace," he explained. "I saw his shoes outside the door this morning and I bagged a bit just in case."

"In case what?"

"In case he should be the murderer, of course. He was the last person to see her and that's always frightfully suspicious, you know. Is it nearly dinner time, do you think? I'm frightfully hungry. It always seems such a long time between tea and dinner. Hallo, there's Uncle Hugo. I didn't know Mums had asked *him* to come down. I suppose she sent for him. She always does if she's in a jam. Here's Josie coming. Hi, Josie!"

Josephine Turner, coming along the terrace, stopped and looked rather startled to see Mrs. Bantry and Miss Marple.

Mrs. Bantry said pleasantly:

"How d'you do, Miss Turner. We've come to do a bit of sleuthing!"

Josie cast a guilty glance round. She said, lowering her voice:

"It's awful. Nobody knows yet. I mean, it isn't in the papers yet. I suppose everyone will be asking me questions and it's so awkward. I don't know what I ought to say."

Her glance went rather wistfully towards Miss Marple, who said: "Yes, it will be a very difficult situation for you, I'm afraid."

Josie warmed to this sympathy.

"You see, Mr. Prestcott said to me: 'Don't talk about it.' And that's all very well, but everyone is sure to ask me, and you can't offend people, can you? Mr. Prestcott said he hoped I'd feel able to carry on as usual—and he wasn't very nice about it, so of course I want to do my best. And I really don't see why it should all be blamed on me."

Sir Henry said:

"Do you mind me asking you a frank question, Miss Turner?"

"Oh, do ask me anything you like," said Josie, a little insincerely.

"Has there been any unpleasantness between

you and Mrs. Jefferson and Mr. Gaskell over all this?"

"Over the murder, do you mean?"

"No, I don't mean the murder."

Josie stood twisting her fingers together. She said rather sullenly:

"Well, there has and there hasn't, if you know what I mean. Neither of them have *said* anything. But I think they blamed it on me—Mr. Jefferson taking such a fancy to Ruby, I mean. It wasn't my fault, though, was it? These things happen, and I never dreamt of such a thing happening beforehand, not for a moment. I—I was quite dumbfounded."

Her words rang out with what seemed undeniable sincerity.

Sir Henry said kindly:

"I'm quite sure you were. But once it *had* happened?"

Josie's chin went up.

"Well, it was a piece of luck, wasn't it? Everyone's got the right to have a piece of luck sometimes."

She looked from one to the other of them in a slightly defiant questioning manner and then went on across the terrace and into the hotel.

Peter said judicially:

"I don't think *she* did it."

Miss Marple murmured:

"It's interesting, that piece of fingernail. It had

been worrying me, you know—how to account for her nails."

"Nails?" asked Sir Henry.

"The dead girl's nails," explained Mrs. Bantry. "They were quite *short,* and now that Jane says so, of course it *was* a little unlikely. A girl like that usually has absolute talons."

Miss Marple said:

"But of course if she tore one off, then she might clip the others close, so as to match. Did they find nail parings in her room, I wonder?"

Sir Henry looked at her curiously. He said:

"I'll ask Superintendent Harper when he gets back."

"Back from where?" asked Mrs. Bantry. "He hasn't gone over to Gossington, has he?"

Sir Henry said gravely:

"No. There's been another tragedy. Blazing car in a quarry—"

Miss Marple caught her breath.

"Was there someone in the car?"

"I'm afraid so—yes."

Miss Marple said thoughtfully:

"I expect that will be the Girl Guide who's missing—Patience—no, Pamela Reeves."

Sir Henry stared at her.

"Now why on earth do you think that, Miss Marple?"

Miss Marple got rather pink.

"Well, it was given out on the wireless that she

145

was missing from her home—since last night. And her home was Daneleigh Vale; that's not very far from here. And she was last seen at the Girl-Guide Rally up on Danebury Downs. That's very close indeed. In fact, she'd have to pass through Danemouth to get home. So it does rather fit in, doesn't it? I mean, it looks as though she might have seen—or perhaps heard—something that no one was supposed to see and hear. If so, of course, she'd be a source of danger to the murderer and she'd have to be—removed. Two things like that *must* be connected, don't you think?"

Sir Henry said, his voice dropping a little:

"You think—a second murder?"

"Why not?" Her quiet placid gaze met his. "When anyone has committed one murder, they don't shrink from another, do they? Nor even from a third."

"A third? You don't think there will be a *third* murder?"

"I think it's just possible . . . Yes, I think it's highly possible."

"Miss Marple," said Sir Henry, "you frighten me. Do you know who is going to be murdered?"

Miss Marple said: "I've a very good idea."

Ten

Superintendent Harper stood looking at the charred and twisted heap of metal. A burnt-up car was always a revolting object, even without the additional gruesome burden of a charred and blackened corpse.

Venn's Quarry was a remote spot, far from any human habitation. Though actually only two miles as the crow flies from Danemouth, the approach to it was by one of those narrow, twisted, rutted roads, little more than a cart track, which led nowhere except to the quarry itself. It was a long time now since the quarry had been worked, and the only people who came along the lane were the casual visitors in search of blackberries. As a spot to dispose of a car it was ideal. The car need not have been found for weeks but for the accident of the glow in the sky having been seen by Albert Biggs, a labourer, on his way to work.

Albert Biggs was still on the scene, though all he had to tell had been heard some time ago, but he continued to repeat the thrilling story with such embellishments as occurred to him.

"Why, dang my eyes, I said, whatever be that? Proper glow it was, up in the sky. Might be a bonfire, I says, but who'd be having bonfire over to Venn's Quarry? No, I says, 'tis some mighty big fire, to be sure. But whatever would it be, I says? There's no house or farm to that direction. 'Tis over by Venn's, I says, that's where it is, to be sure. Didn't rightly know what I ought to do about it, but seeing as Constable Gregg comes along just then on his bicycle, I tells him about it. 'Twas all died down by then, but I tells him just where 'twere. 'Tis over that direction, I says. Big glare in the sky, I says. Mayhap as it's a rick, I says. One of them tramps, as likely as not, set alight of it. But I did never think as how it might be a car—far less as someone was being burnt up alive in it. 'Tis a terrible tragedy, to be sure."

The Glenshire police had been busy. Cameras had clicked and the position of the charred body had been carefully noted before the police surgeon had started his own investigation.

The latter came over now to Harper, dusting black ash off his hands, his lips set grimly together.

"A pretty thorough job," he said. "Part of one foot and shoe are about all that has escaped. Personally I myself couldn't say if the body was a man's or a woman's at the moment, though we'll get some indication from the bones, I expect. But the shoe is one of the black strapped affairs—the kind schoolgirls wear."

"There's a schoolgirl missing from the next county," said Harper; "quite close to here. Girl of sixteen or so."

"Then it's probably her," said the doctor. "Poor kid."

Harper said uneasily: "She wasn't alive when—?"

"No, no, I don't think so. No signs of her having tried to get out. Body was just slumped down on the seat—with the foot sticking out. She was dead when she was put there, I should say. Then the car was set fire to in order to try and get rid of the evidence."

He paused, and asked:

"Want me any longer?"

"I don't think so, thank you."

"Right. I'll be off."

He strode away to his car. Harper went over to where one of his sergeants, a man who specialized in car cases, was busy.

The latter looked up.

"Quite a clear case, sir. Petrol poured over the car and the whole thing deliberately set light to. There are three empty cans in the hedge over there."

A little farther away another man was carefully arranging small objects picked out of the wreckage. There was a scorched black leather shoe and with it some scraps of scorched and blackened material. As Harper approached, his subordinate looked up and exclaimed:

"Look at this, sir. This seems to clinch it."

Harper took the small object in his hand. He said:

"Button from a Girl Guide's uniform?"

"Yes, sir."

"Yes," said Harper, "that does seem to settle it."

A decent, kindly man, he felt slightly sick. First Ruby Keene and now this child, Pamela Reeves.

He said to himself, as he had said before:

"What's come to Glenshire?"

His next move was first to ring up his own Chief Constable, and afterwards to get in touch with Colonel Melchett. The disappearance of Pamela Reeves had taken place in Radfordshire though her body had been found in Glenshire.

The next task set him was not a pleasant one. He had to break the news to Pamela Reeves's father and mother. . . .

II

Superintendent Harper looked up consideringly at the façade of Braeside as he rang the front door bell.

Neat little villa, nice garden of about an acre and a half. The sort of place that had been built fairly freely all over the countryside in the last twenty years. Retired Army men, retired Civil Servants—that type. Nice decent folk; the worst you could say of them was that they might be a bit dull. Spent as much money as they could afford on their children's education. Not the kind of people you associated with tragedy. And now tragedy had come to them. He sighed.

He was shown at once into a lounge where a stiff man with a grey moustache and a woman whose eyes were red with weeping both sprang up. Mrs. Reeves cried out eagerly:

"You have some news of Pamela?"

Then she shrank back, as though the Superintendent's commiserating glance had been a blow.

Harper said:

"I'm afraid you must prepare yourself for bad news."

"Pamela—" faltered the woman.

Major Reeves said sharply:

"Something's happened—to the child?"

"Yes, sir."

"Do you mean she's dead?"

Mrs. Reeves burst out:

"Oh no, no," and broke into a storm of weeping. Major Reeves put his arm round his wife and drew her to him. His lips trembled but he looked inquiringly at Harper, who bent his head.

"An accident?"

"Not exactly, Major Reeves. She was found in a burnt-out car which had been abandoned in a quarry."

"In a car? In a quarry?"

His astonishment was evident.

Mrs. Reeves broke down altogether and sank down on the sofa, sobbing violently.

Superintendent Harper said:

"If you'd like me to wait a few minutes?"

Major Reeves said sharply:

"What does this mean? Foul play?"

"That's what it looks like, sir. That's why I'd like to ask you some questions if it isn't too trying for you."

"No, no, you're quite right. No time must be lost if what you suggest is true. But I can't believe it. Who would want to harm a child like Pamela?"

Harper said stolidly:

"You've already reported to your local police the circumstances of your daughter's disappearance. She left here to attend a Guides rally and you expected her home for supper. That is right?"

"Yes."

"She was to return by bus?"

"Yes."

"I understand that, according to the story of her fellow Guides, when the rally was over Pamela said she was going into Danemouth to Woolworth's, and would catch a later bus home. That strikes you as quite a normal proceeding?"

"Oh yes, Pamela was very fond of going to Woolworth's. She often went into Danemouth to shop. The bus goes from the main road, only about a quarter of a mile from here."

"And she had no other plans, so far as you know?"

"None."

"She was not meeting anybody in Danemouth?"

"No, I'm sure she wasn't. She would have mentioned it if so. We expected her back for supper. That's why, when it got so late and she hadn't turned up, we rang up the police. It wasn't like her not to come home."

"Your daughter had no undesirable friends— that is, friends that you didn't approve of?"

"No, there was never any trouble of that kind."

Mrs. Reeves said tearfully:

"Pam was just a child. She was very young for her age. She liked games and all that. She wasn't precocious in any way."

"Do you know a Mr. George Bartlett who is staying at the Majestic Hotel in Danemouth?"

Major Reeves stared.

"Never heard of him."

"You don't think your daughter knew him?"

"I'm quite sure she didn't."

He added sharply: "How does he come into it?"

"He's the owner of the Minoan 14 car in which your daughter's body was found."

Mrs. Reeves cried: "But then he must—"

Harper said quickly:

"He reported his car missing early today. It was in the courtyard of the Majestic Hotel at lunch time yesterday. Anybody might have taken the car."

"But didn't someone see who took it?"

The Superintendent shook his head.

"Dozens of cars going in and out all day. And a Minoan 14 is one of the commonest makes."

Mrs. Reeves cried:

"But aren't you doing something? Aren't you trying to find the—the devil who did this? My little girl—oh, my little girl! She wasn't burnt alive, was she? Oh, Pam, Pam . . . !"

"She didn't suffer, Mrs. Reeves. I assure you she was already dead when the car was set alight."

Reeves asked stiffly:

"How was she killed?"

Harper gave him a significant glance.

"We don't know. The fire had destroyed all evidence of that kind."

He turned to the distraught woman on the sofa.

"Believe me, Mrs. Reeves, we're doing everything we can. It's a matter of checking up. Sooner or later we shall find someone who saw your daughter in Danemouth yesterday, and saw whom she was with. It all takes time, you know. We shall have dozens, hundreds of reports coming in about a Girl Guide who was seen here, there, and everywhere. It's a matter of selection and of patience—but we shall find out the truth in the end, never you fear."

Mrs. Reeves asked:

"Where—where is she? Can I go to her?"

Again Superintendent Harper caught the husband's eye. He said:

"The medical officer is attending to all that. I'd suggest that your husband comes with me now and attends to all the formalities. In the meantime, try and recollect anything Pamela may have said—something, perhaps, that you didn't pay attention to at the time but which might throw some light upon things. You know what I mean— just some chance word or phrase. That's the best way you can help us."

As the two men went towards the door, Reeves said, pointing to a photograph:

"There she is."

Harper looked at it attentively. It was a hockey group. Reeves pointed out Pamela in the centre of the team.

"A nice kid," Harper thought, as he looked at the earnest face of the pigtailed girl.

His mouth set in a grim line as he thought of the charred body in the car.

He vowed to himself that the murder of Pamela Reeves should not remain one of Glenshire's unsolved mysteries.

Ruby Keene, so he admitted privately, might have asked for what was coming to her, but Pamela Reeves was quite another story. A nice kid, if he ever saw one. He'd not rest until he'd hunted down the man or woman who'd killed her.

Eleven

A day or two later Colonel Melchett and Superintendent Harper looked at each other across the former's big desk. Harper had come over to Much Benham for a consultation.

Melchett said gloomily:

"Well, we know where we are—or rather where we aren't!"

"Where we aren't expresses it better, sir."

"We've got two deaths to take into account," said Melchett. "Two murders. Ruby Keene and the child Pamela Reeves. Not much to identify her by, poor kid, but enough. That shoe that escaped burning has been identified positively as hers by her father, and there's this button from her Girl Guide uniform. A fiendish business, Superintendent."

Superintendent Harper said very quietly:

"I'll say you're right, sir."

"I'm glad it's quite certain she was dead before the car was set on fire. The way she was lying, thrown across the seat, shows that. Probably knocked on the head, poor kid."

"Or strangled, perhaps," said Harper.

Melchett looked at him sharply.

"You think so?"

"Well, sir, there are murderers like that."

"I know. I've seen the parents—the poor girl's

mother's beside herself. Damned painful, the whole thing. The point for us to settle is—are the two murders connected?"

"I'd say definitely yes."

"So would I."

The Superintendent ticked off the points on his fingers.

"Pamela Reeves attended rally of Girl Guides on Danebury Downs. Stated by companions to be normal and cheerful. Did not return with three companions by the bus to Medchester. Said to them that she was going into Danemouth to Woolworth's and would take the bus home from there. The main road into Danemouth from the downs does a big round inland. Pamela Reeves took a shortcut over two fields and a footpath and lane which would bring her into Danemouth near the Majestic Hotel. The lane, in fact, actually passes the hotel on the west side. It's possible, therefore, that she overheard or saw something—something concerning Ruby Keene—which would have proved dangerous to the murderer—say, for instance, that she heard him arranging to meet Ruby Keene at eleven that evening. He realizes that this schoolgirl has overheard, and he has to silence her."

Colonel Melchett said:

"That's presuming, Harper, that the Ruby Keene crime was premeditated—not spontaneous."

Superintendent Harper agreed.

"I believe it was, sir. It looks as though it would be the other way—sudden violence, a fit of passion or jealousy—but I'm beginning to think that that's not so. I don't see otherwise how you can account for the death of the Reeves child. If she was a witness of the actual crime, it would be late at night, round about eleven p.m., and what would she be doing round about the Majestic at that time? Why, at nine o'clock her parents were getting anxious because she hadn't returned."

"The alternative is that she went to meet someone in Danemouth unknown to her family and friends, and that her death is quite unconnected with the other death."

"Yes, sir, and I don't believe that's so. Look how even the old lady, old Miss Marple, tumbled to it at once that there was a connection. She asked at once if the body in the burnt car was the body of the missing Girl Guide. Very smart old lady, that. These old ladies are sometimes. Shrewd, you know. Put their fingers on the vital spot."

"Miss Marple has done that more than once," said Colonel Melchett dryly.

"And besides, sir, there's the car. That seems to me to link up her death definitely with the Majestic Hotel. It was Mr. George Bartlett's car."

Again the eyes of the two men met. Melchett said:

"George Bartlett? Could be! What do you think?"

Again Harper methodically recited various points.

"Ruby Keene was last seen with George Bartlett. He says she went to her room (borne out by the dress she was wearing being found there), but did she go to her room and change *in order to go out with him?* Had they made a date to go out together earlier—discussed it, say, before dinner, and did Pamela Reeves happen to overhear?"

Melchett said: "He didn't report the loss of his car until the following morning, and he was extremely vague about it then, pretended he couldn't remember exactly when he had last noticed it."

"That might be cleverness, sir. As I see it, he's either a very clever gentleman pretending to be a silly ass, or else—well, he is a silly ass."

"What we want," said Melchett, "is motive. As it stands, he had no motive whatever for killing Ruby Keene."

"Yes—that's where we're stuck every time. Motive. All the reports from the Palais de Danse at Brixwell are negative, I understand?"

"Absolutely! Ruby Keene had no special boy friend. Slack's been into the matter thoroughly— give Slack his due, he *is* thorough."

"That's right, sir. Thorough's the word."

"If there was anything to ferret out, he'd have

159

ferreted it out. But there's nothing there. He got a list of her most frequent dancing partners—all vetted and found correct. Harmless fellows, and all able to produce alibis for that night."

"Ah," said Superintendent Harper. "Alibis. That's what we're up against."

Melchett looked at him sharply. "Think so? I've left that side of the investigation to you."

"Yes, sir. It's been gone into—very thoroughly. We applied to London for help over it."

"Well?"

"Mr. Conway Jefferson may think that Mr. Gaskell and young Mrs. Jefferson are comfortably off, but that is not the case. They're both extremely hard up."

"Is that true?"

"Quite true, sir. It's as Mr. Conway Jefferson said, he made over considerable sums of money to his son and daughter when they married. That was over ten years ago, though. Mr. Jefferson fancied himself as knowing good investments. He didn't invest in anything absolutely wild cat, but he was unlucky and showed poor judgment more than once. His holdings have gone steadily down. I should say the widow found it difficult to make both ends meet and send her son to a good school."

"But she hasn't applied to her father-in-law for help?"

"No, sir. As far as I can make out she lives with

him, and consequently has no household expenses."

"And his health is such that he wasn't expected to live long?"

"That's right, sir. Now for Mr. Mark Gaskell. He's a gambler, pure and simple. Got through his wife's money very soon. Has got himself tangled up rather critically just at present. He needs money badly—and a good deal of it."

"Can't say I liked the looks of him much," said Colonel Melchett. "Wild-looking sort of fellow— what? And he's got a motive all right. Twenty-five thousand pounds it meant to him getting that girl out of the way. Yes, it's a motive all right."

"They both had a motive."

"I'm not considering Mrs. Jefferson."

"No, sir, I know you're not. And, anyway, the alibi holds for both of them. They *couldn't* have done it. Just that."

"You've got a detailed statement of their movements that evening?"

"Yes, I have. Take Mr. Gaskell first. He dined with his father-in-law and Mrs. Jefferson, had coffee with them afterwards when Ruby Keene joined them. Then he said he had to write letters and left them. Actually he took his car and went for a spin down to the front. He told me quite frankly he couldn't stick playing bridge for a whole evening. The old boy's mad on it. So he made letters an excuse. Ruby Keene remained with the others. Mark Gaskell returned when she was dancing with Raymond. After the dance Ruby came and had a drink with them, then she went off with young Bartlett, and Gaskell and the others cut for partners and started their bridge. That was at twenty minutes to eleven—and he didn't leave the table until after midnight. That's quite certain, sir. Everyone says so. The family, the waiters, everyone. Therefore *he* couldn't have done it. And Mrs. Jefferson's alibi is the same. She, too, didn't leave the table. They're out, both of them—out."

Colonel Melchett leaned back, tapping the table with a paper cutter.

Superintendent Harper said:

"That is, assuming the girl was killed before midnight."

"Haydock said she was. He's a very sound fellow in police work. If he says a thing, it's so."

"There might be reasons—health, physical idiosyncrasy, or something."

"I'll put it to him." Melchett glanced at his watch, picked up the telephone receiver and asked for a number. He said: "Haydock ought to be at home at this time. Now, assuming that she was killed *after* midnight?"

Harper said:

"Then there might be a chance. There was some coming and going afterwards. Let's assume that Gaskell had asked the girl to meet him outside somewhere—say at twenty past twelve. He slips away for a minute or two, strangles her, comes back and disposes of the body later—in the early hours of the morning."

Melchett said:

"Takes her by car thirty-odd miles to put her in Bantry's library? Dash it all, it's not a likely story."

"No, it isn't," the Superintendent admitted at once.

The telephone rang. Melchett picked up the receiver.

"Hallo, Haydock, is that you? Ruby Keene. Would it be possible for her to have been killed *after* midnight?"

"I told you she was killed between ten and midnight."

"Yes, I know, but one could stretch it a bit—what?"

"No, you couldn't stretch it. When I say she was killed before midnight I mean before midnight, and don't try to tamper with the medical evidence."

"Yes, but couldn't there be some physiological what-not? You know what I mean."

"I know that you don't know what you're talking about. The girl was perfectly healthy and not abnormal in any way—and I'm not going to say she was just to help you fit a rope round the neck of some wretched fellow whom you police wallahs have got your knife into. Now don't protest. I know your ways. And, by the way, the girl wasn't strangled willingly—that is to say, she was drugged first. Powerful narcotic. She died of strangulation but she was drugged first." Haydock rang off.

Melchett said gloomily: "Well, that's that."

Harper said:

"Thought I'd found another likely starter—but it petered out."

"What's that? Who?"

"Strictly speaking, he's your pigeon, sir. Name of Basil Blake. Lives near Gossington Hall."

"Impudent young jackanapes!" The Colonel's brow darkened as he remembered Basil Blake's outrageous rudeness. "How's he mixed up in it?"

"Seems he knew Ruby Keene. Dined over at the Majestic quite often—danced with the girl. Do you remember what Josie said to Raymond when Ruby was discovered to be missing? 'She's not with that film fellow, is she?' I've found out it was Blake, she meant. He's employed with the Lemville Studios, you know. Josie has nothing to go upon except a belief that Ruby was rather keen on him."

"Very promising, Harper, very promising."

"Not so good as it sounds, sir. Basil Blake was at a party at the studios that night. You know the sort of thing. Starts at eight with cocktails and goes on and on until the air's too thick to see

164

through and everyone passes out. According to Inspector Slack, who's questioned him, he left the show round about midnight. At midnight Ruby Keene was dead."

"Anyone bear out his statement?"

"Most of them, I gather, sir, were rather—er—far gone. The—er—young woman now at the bungalow—Miss Dinah Lee—says his statement is correct."

"Doesn't mean a thing!"

"No, sir, probably not. Statements taken from other members of the party bear Mr. Blake's statement out on the whole, though ideas as to time are somewhat vague."

"Where are these studios?"

"Lemville, sir, thirty miles southwest of London."

"H'm—about the same distance from here?"

"Yes, sir."

Colonel Melchett rubbed his nose. He said in a rather dissatisfied tone:

"Well, it looks as though we could wash him out."

"I think so, sir. There is no evidence that he was seriously attracted by Ruby Keene. In fact"—Superintendent Harper coughed primly—"he seems fully occupied with his own young lady."

Melchett said:

"Well, we are left with 'X,' an unknown murderer—so unknown Slack can't find a trace of him! Or Jefferson's son-in-law, who might have wanted to kill the girl—but didn't have a chance to do so. Daughter-in-law ditto. Or George Bartlett, who has no alibi—but unfortunately no motive either. Or with young Blake, who has an alibi and no motive. And that's the lot! No, stop, I suppose we ought to consider the dancing fellow—Raymond Starr. After all, he saw a lot of the girl."

Harper said slowly:

"Can't believe he took much interest in her—or else he's a thundering good actor. And, for all practical purposes, he's got an alibi too. He was more or less in view from twenty minutes to eleven until midnight, dancing with various partners. I don't see that we can make a case against him."

"In fact," said Colonel Melchett, "we can't make a case against anybody."

"George Bartlett's our best hope. If we could only hit on a motive."

"You've had him looked up?"

"Yes, sir. Only child. Coddled by his mother. Came into a good deal of money on her death a year ago. Getting through it fast. Weak rather than vicious."

"May be mental," said Melchett hopefully.

Superintendent Harper nodded. He said:

"Has it struck you, sir—that that may be the explanation of the whole case?"

"Criminal lunatic, you mean?"

"Yes, sir. One of those fellows who go about strangling young girls. Doctors have a long name for it."

"That would solve all our difficulties," said Melchett.

"There's only one thing I don't like about it," said Superintendent Harper.

"What?"

"It's too easy."

"H'm—yes—perhaps. So, as I said at the beginning where are we?"

"Nowhere, sir," said Superintendent Harper.

Twelve

Conway Jefferson stirred in his sleep and stretched. His arms were flung out, long, powerful arms into which all the strength of his body seemed to be concentrated since his accident.

Through the curtains the morning light glowed softly.

Conway Jefferson smiled to himself. Always, after a night of rest, he woke like this, happy, refreshed, his deep vitality renewed. Another day!

So for a minute he lay. Then he pressed the special bell by his hand. And suddenly a wave of remembrance swept over him.

Even as Edwards, deft and quiet-footed, entered the room, a groan was wrung from his master.

Edwards paused with his hand on the curtains. He said: "You're not in pain, sir?"

Conway Jefferson said harshly:

"No. Go on, pull 'em."

The clear light flooded the room. Edwards, understanding, did not glance at his master.

His face grim, Conway Jefferson lay remembering and thinking. Before his eyes he saw again the pretty, vapid face of Ruby. Only in his mind he did not use the adjective vapid. Last night he would have said innocent. A naïve, innocent child! And now?

A great weariness came over Conway Jefferson. He closed his eyes. He murmured below his breath:

"Margaret. . . ."

It was the name of his dead wife. . . .

II

"I like your friend," said Adelaide Jefferson to Mrs. Bantry.

The two women were sitting on the terrace.

"Jane Marple's a very remarkable woman," said Mrs. Bantry.

"She's nice too," said Addie, smiling.

"People call her a scandalmonger," said Mrs. Bantry, "but she isn't really."

"Just a low opinion of human nature?"

"You could call it that."

"It's rather refreshing," said Adelaide Jefferson, "after having had too much of the other thing."

Mrs. Bantry looked at her sharply.

Addie explained herself.

"So much high-thinking—idealization of an unworthy object!"

"You mean Ruby Keene?"

Addie nodded.

"I don't want to be horrid about her. There wasn't any harm in her. Poor little rat, she had to fight for what she wanted. She wasn't bad. Common and rather silly and quite good-natured, but a decided little gold-digger. I don't think she schemed or planned. It was just that she was quick to take advantage of a possibility. And she knew just how to appeal to an elderly man who was—lonely."

"I suppose," said Mrs. Bantry thoughtfully, "that Conway *was* lonely?"

Addie moved restlessly. She said:

"He was—this summer." She paused and then burst out: "Mark will have it that it was all my fault. Perhaps it was, I don't know."

She was silent for a minute, then, impelled by some need to talk, she went on speaking in a difficult, almost reluctant way.

"I—I've had such an odd sort of life. Mike Carmody, my first husband, died so soon after we were married—it—it knocked me out. Peter, as you know, was born after his death. Frank Jefferson was Mike's great friend. So I came to see a lot of him. He was Peter's godfather—Mike had wanted that. I got very fond of him—and—oh! sorry for him too."

"Sorry?" queried Mrs. Bantry with interest.

"Yes, just that. It sounds odd. Frank had always had everything he wanted. His father and his mother couldn't have been nicer to him. And yet—how can I say it?—you see, old Mr. Jefferson's personality is so strong. If you live with it, you can't somehow have a personality of your own. Frank felt that.

170

"When we were married he was very happy—wonderfully so. Mr. Jefferson was very generous. He settled a large sum of money on Frank—said he wanted his children to be independent and not have to wait for his death. It was so nice of him—so generous. But it was much too sudden. He ought really to have accustomed Frank to independence little by little.

"It went to Frank's head. He wanted to be as good a man as his father, as clever about money and business, as far-seeing and successful. And, of course, he wasn't. He didn't exactly speculate with the money, but he invested in the wrong things at the wrong time. It's frightening, you know, how soon money goes if you're not clever about it. The more Frank dropped, the more eager he was to get it back by some clever deal. So things went from bad to worse."

"But, my dear," said Mrs. Bantry, "couldn't Conway have advised him?"

"He didn't want to be advised. The one thing he wanted was to do well on his own. That's why we never let Mr. Jefferson know. When Frank died there was very little left—only a tiny income for me. And I—I didn't let his father know either. You see—"

She turned abruptly.

"It would have felt like betraying Frank to him. Frank would have hated it so. Mr. Jefferson was ill for a long time. When he got well he assumed that

I was a very-well-off widow. I've never undeceived him. It's been a point of honour. He knows I'm very careful about money—but he approves of that, thinks I'm a thrifty sort of woman. And, of course, Peter and I have lived with him practically ever since, and he's paid for all our living expenses. So I've never had to worry."

She said slowly:

"We've been like a family all these years—only—only—you see (or don't you see?) I've never been Frank's *widow* to him—I've been Frank's *wife*."

Mrs. Bantry grasped the implication.

"You mean he's never accepted their deaths?"

"No. He's been wonderful. But he's conquered his own terrible tragedy by refusing to recognize death. Mark is Rosamund's husband and I'm Frank's wife—and though Frank and Rosamund aren't exactly here with us—they are still existent."

Mrs. Bantry said softly:

"It's a wonderful triumph of faith."

"I know. We've gone on, year after year. But suddenly—this summer—something went wrong in me. I felt—I felt rebellious. It's an awful thing to say, but I didn't want to think of Frank anymore! All that was over—my love and companionship with him, and my grief when he died. It was something that had been and wasn't any longer.

"It's awfully hard to describe. It's like wanting to wipe the slate clean and start again. I wanted to be me—Addie, still reasonably young and strong and able to play games and swim and dance—just a *person*. Even Hugo—(you know Hugo McLean?) he's a dear and wants to marry me, but, of course, I've never really thought of it—but this summer I *did* begin to think of it—not seriously—only vaguely. . . ."

She stopped and shook her head.

"And so I suppose it's true. *I neglected Jeff.* I don't mean *really* neglected him, but my mind and thoughts weren't with him. When Ruby, as I saw, amused him, I was rather glad. It left me freer to go and do my own things. I never dreamed—of course I never dreamed—that he would be so—so—*infatuated* by her!"

Mrs. Bantry asked:

"And when you did find out?"

"I was dumbfounded—absolutely dumbfounded! And, I'm afraid, angry too."

"*I*'d have been angry," said Mrs. Bantry.

"There was Peter, you see. Peter's whole future depends on Jeff. Jeff practically looked on him as a grandson, or so I thought, but, of course, he wasn't a grandson. He was no relation at all. And to think that he was going to be—disinherited!" Her firm, well-shaped hands shook a little where they lay in her lap. "For that's what it felt like—and for a vulgar, gold-digging little simpleton—Oh! I could have killed her!"

She stopped, stricken. Her beautiful hazel eyes met Mrs. Bantry's in a pleading horror. She said:

"What an awful thing to say!"

Hugo McLean, coming quietly up behind them, asked:

"What's an awful thing to say?"

"Sit down, Hugo. You know Mrs. Bantry, don't you?"

McLean had already greeted the older lady. He said now in a low, persevering way:

"What was an awful thing to say?"

Addie Jefferson said:

"That I'd like to have killed Ruby Keene."

Hugo McLean reflected a minute or two. Then he said:

"No, I wouldn't say that if I were you. Might be misunderstood." His eyes—steady, reflective, grey eyes—looked at her meaningly.

He said:

"You've got to watch your step, Addie."

There was a warning in his voice.

III

When Miss Marple came out of the hotel and joined Mrs. Bantry a few minutes later, Hugo McLean and Adelaide Jefferson were walking down the path to the sea together.

Seating herself, Miss Marple remarked:

"He seems very devoted."

"He's been devoted for years! One of those men."

"I know. Like Major Bury. He hung round an Anglo-Indian widow for quite ten years. A joke among her friends! In the end she gave in—but unfortunately ten days before they were to have been married she ran away with the chauffeur! Such a nice woman, too, and usually so well balanced."

"People do do very odd things," agreed Mrs. Bantry. "I wish you'd been here just now, Jane. Addie Jefferson was telling me all about herself—how her husband went through all his money but they never let Mr. Jefferson know. And then, this summer, things felt different to her—"

Miss Marple nodded.

"Yes. She rebelled, I suppose, against being made to live in the past? After all, there's a time for everything. You can't sit in the house with the blinds down forever. I suppose Mrs. Jefferson just pulled them up and took off her widow's weeds, and her father-in-law, of course, didn't like it. Felt left out in the cold, though I don't suppose for a minute he realized who put her up to it. Still, he certainly wouldn't like it. And so, of course, like old Mr. Badger when his wife took up Spiritualism, he was just ripe for what happened. Any fairly nice-looking young girl who listened prettily would have done."

"Do you think," said Mrs. Bantry, "that that cousin, Josie, got her down here deliberately—that it was a family plot?"

Miss Marple shook her head.

"No, I don't think so at all. I don't think Josie has the kind of mind that could foresee people's reactions. She's rather dense in that way. She's got one of those shrewd, limited, practical minds that never do foresee the future and are usually astonished by it."

"It seems to have taken everyone by surprise," said Mrs. Bantry. "Addie—and Mark Gaskell too, apparently."

Miss Marple smiled.

"I dare say he had his own fish to fry. A bold fellow with a roving eye! Not the man to go on being a sorrowing widower for years, no matter how fond he may have been of his wife. I should think they were both restless under old Mr. Jefferson's yoke of perpetual remembrance.

"Only," added Miss Marple cynically, "it's easier for gentlemen, of course."

IV

At that very moment Mark was confirming this judgment on himself in a talk with Sir Henry Clithering.

With characteristic candour Mark had gone straight to the heart of things.

"It's just dawned on me," he said, "that I'm Favourite Suspect No. I to the police! They've been delving into my financial troubles. I'm broke, you know, or very nearly. If dear old Jeff dies according to schedule in a month or two, and Addie and I divide the dibs also according to schedule, all will be well. Matter of fact, I owe rather a lot . . . If the crash comes it will be a big one! If I can stave it off, it will be the other way round—I shall come out on top and be a very rich man."

Sir Henry Clithering said:

"You're a gambler, Mark."

"Always have been. Risk everything—that's my motto! Yes, it's a lucky thing for me that somebody strangled that poor kid. I didn't do it. I'm not a strangler. I don't really think I could ever murder anybody. I'm too easygoing. But I don't suppose I can ask the police to believe *that!* I must look to them like the answer to the criminal investigator's prayer! I had a motive, was on the spot, I am not burdened with high moral scruples! I can't imagine why I'm not in the jug already! That Superintendent's got a very nasty eye."

"You've got that useful thing, an alibi."

"An alibi is the fishiest thing on God's earth! No innocent person ever has an alibi! Besides, it all depends on the time of death, or something like that, and you may be sure if three doctors say the girl was killed at midnight, at least six will be found who will swear positively that she was killed at five in the morning—and where's my alibi then?"

"At any rate, you are able to joke about it."

"Damned bad taste, isn't it?" said Mark cheerfully. "Actually, I'm rather scared. One is—with murder! And don't think I'm not sorry for old Jeff. I am. But it's better this way—bad as the shock was—than if he'd found her out."

"What do you mean, found her out?"

Mark winked.

"Where did she go off to last night? I'll lay you any odds you like she went to meet a man. Jeff wouldn't have liked that. He wouldn't have liked it at all. If he'd found she was deceiving him—that she wasn't the prattling little innocent she seemed—well—my father-in-law is an odd man. He's a man of great self-control, but that self-control can snap. And then—look out!"

Sir Henry glanced at him curiously.

"Are you fond of him or not?"

"I'm very fond of him—and at the same time I resent him. I'll try and explain. Conway Jefferson is a man who likes to control his surroundings. He's a benevolent despot, kind, generous, and affectionate—but his is the tune, and the others dance to his piping."

Mark Gaskell paused.

"I loved my wife. I shall never feel the same for

anyone else. Rosamund was sunshine and laughter and flowers, and when she was killed I felt just like a man in the ring who's had a knockout blow. But the referee's been counting a good long time now. I'm a man, after all. I like women. I don't want to marry again—not in the least. Well, that's all right. I've had to be discreet—but I've had my good times all right. Poor Addie hasn't. Addie's a really nice woman. She's the kind of woman men want to marry, not to sleep with. Give her half a chance and she would marry again—and be very happy and make the chap happy too. But old Jeff saw her always as Frank's wife—and hypnotized her into seeing herself like that. He doesn't know it, but we've been in prison. I broke out, on the quiet, a long time ago. Addie broke out this summer—and it gave him a shock. It split up his world. Result—Ruby Keene."

Irrepressibly he sang:

"But she is in her grave, and, oh,
The difference to me!

"Come and have a drink, Clithering."

It was hardly surprising, Sir Henry reflected, that Mark Gaskell should be an object of suspicion to the police.

Thirteen

Dr. Metcalf was one of the best-known physicians in Danemouth. He had no aggressive bedside manner, but his presence in the sick room had an invariably cheering effect. He was middle-aged, with a quiet pleasant voice.

He listened carefully to Superintendent Harper and replied to his questions with gentle precision.

Harper said:

"Then I can take it, Doctor Metcalf, that what I was told by Mrs. Jefferson was substantially correct?"

"Yes, Mr. Jefferson's health is in a precarious state. For several years now the man has been driving himself ruthlessly. In his determination to live like other men, he has lived at a far greater pace than the normal man of his age. He has refused to rest, to take things easy, to go slow—or any of the other phrases with which I and his other medical advisers have tendered our opinion. The result is that the man is an overworked engine. Heart, lungs, blood pressure—they're all overstrained."

"You say Mr. Jefferson has absolutely refused to listen?"

"Yes. I don't know that I blame him. It's not what I say to my patients, Superintendent, but a man may as well wear out as rust out. A lot of my colleagues do that, and take it from me it's not a bad way. In a place like Danemouth one sees most of the other thing: invalids clinging to life, terrified of over-exerting themselves, terrified of a breath of draughty air, of a stray germ, of an injudicious meal!"

"I expect that's true enough," said Superintendent Harper. "What it amounts to, then, is this: Conway Jefferson is strong enough, physically speaking—or, I suppose I mean, muscularly speaking. Just what can he do in the active line, by the way?"

"He has immense strength in his arms and shoulders. He was a powerful man before his accident. He is extremely dexterous in his handling of his wheeled chair, and with the aid of crutches he can move himself about a room— from his bed to the chair, for instance."

"Isn't it possible for a man injured as Mr. Jefferson was to have artificial legs?"

"Not in his case. There was a spine injury."

"I see. Let me sum up again. Jefferson is strong and fit in the muscular sense. He feels well and all that?"

Metcalf nodded.

"But his heart is in a bad condition. Any overstrain or exertion, or a shock or a sudden fright, and he might pop off. Is that it?"

"More or less. Over-exertion is killing him slowly, because he won't give in when he feels tired. That aggravates the cardiac condition. It is unlikely that exertion would kill him suddenly. But a sudden shock or fright might easily do so. That is why I expressly warned his family."

Superintendent Harper said slowly:

"But in actual fact a shock *didn't* kill him. I mean, doctor, that there couldn't have been a much worse shock than this business, and he's still alive?"

Dr. Metcalf shrugged his shoulders.

"I know. But if you'd had my experience, Superintendent, you'd know that case history shows the impossibility of prognosticating accurately. People who *ought* to die of shock and exposure *don't* die of shock and exposure, etc., etc. The human frame is tougher than one can imagine possible. Moreover, in my experience, a *physical* shock is more often fatal than a *mental* shock. In plain language, a door banging suddenly would be more likely to kill Mr. Jefferson than the discovery that a girl he was fond of had died in a particularly horrible manner."

"Why is that, I wonder?"

"The breaking of a piece of bad news nearly always sets up a defence reaction. It numbs the recipient. They are unable—at first—to take it in. Full realization takes a little time. But the banged door, someone jumping out of a cupboard, the sudden onslaught of a motor as you cross a road—all those things are immediate in their action. The heart gives a terrified leap—to put it in layman's language."

Superintendent Harper said slowly:

"But as far as anyone would know, Mr. Jefferson's death might easily have been caused by the shock of the girl's death?"

"Oh, easily." The doctor looked curiously at the other. "You don't think—"

"I don't know what I think," said Superintendent Harper vexedly.

II

"But you'll admit, sir, that the two things would fit in very prettily together," he said a little later to Sir Henry Clithering. "Kill two birds with one stone. First the girl—and the fact of her death takes off Mr. Jefferson too—before he's had any opportunity of altering his will."

"Do you think he will alter it?"

"You'd be more likely to know that, sir, than I would. What do you say?"

"I don't know. Before Ruby Keene came on the scene I happen to know that he had left his money between Mark Gaskell and Mrs. Jefferson. I don't see why he should now change his mind about that. But of course he might do so. Might leave it to a Cats' Home, or to subsidize young professional dancers."

Superintendent Harper agreed.

"You never know what bee a man is going to get in his bonnet—especially when he doesn't feel there's any moral obligation in the disposal of his fortune. No blood relations in this case."

Sir Henry said:

"He is fond of the boy—of young Peter."

"D'you think he regards him as a grandson? You'd know that better than I would, sir."

Sir Henry said slowly:

"No, I don't think so."

"There's another thing I'd like to ask you, sir. It's a thing I can't judge for myself. But they're friends of yours and so you'd know. I'd like very much to know just how fond Mr. Jefferson is of Mr. Gaskell and young Mrs. Jefferson."

Sir Henry frowned.

"I'm not sure if I understand you, Superintendent?"

"Well, it's this way, sir. How fond is he of them as *persons*—apart from his relationship to them?"

"Ah, I see what you mean."

"Yes, sir. Nobody doubts that he was very attached to them both—but he was attached to them, as I see it, because they were, respectively, the husband and the wife of his daughter and his son. But supposing, for instance, one of them had married again?"

Sir Henry reflected. He said:

"It's an interesting point you raise there. I don't

184

know. I'm inclined to suspect—this is a mere opinion—that it would have altered his attitude a good deal. He would have wished them well, borne no rancour, but I think, yes, I rather think that he would have taken very little more interest in them."

"In both cases, sir?"

"I think so, yes. In Mr. Gaskell's, almost certainly, and I rather think in Mrs. Jefferson's also, but that's not nearly so certain. I think he *was* fond of her for her own sake."

"Sex would have something to do with that," said Superintendent Harper sapiently. "Easier for him to look on her as a daughter than to look on Mr. Gaskell as a son. It works both ways. Women accept a son-in-law as one of the family easily enough, but there aren't many times when a woman looks on her son's wife as a daughter."

Superintendent Harper went on:

"Mind if we walk along this path, sir, to the tennis court? I see Miss Marple's sitting there. I want to ask her to do something for me. As a matter of fact I want to rope you both in."

"In what way, Superintendent?"

"To get at stuff that I can't get at myself. I want you to tackle Edwards for me, sir."

"Edwards? What do you want from him?"

"Everything you can think of! Everything he knows and what he thinks! About the relations between the various members of the family, his angle on the Ruby Keene business. Inside stuff. He knows better than anyone the state of affairs—you bet he does! And he wouldn't tell *me*. But he'll tell *you*. And something *might* turn up from it. That is, of course, if you don't object?"

Sir Henry said grimly:

"I don't object. I've been sent for, urgently, to get at the truth. I mean to do my utmost."

He added:

"How do you want Miss Marple to help you?"

"With some girls. Some of those Girl Guides. We've rounded up half a dozen or so, the ones who were most friendly with Pamela Reeves. It's possible that they may know something. You see, I've been thinking. It seems to me that if that girl was really going to Woolworth's she would have tried to persuade one of the other girls to go with her. Girls usually like to shop with someone."

"Yes, I think that's true."

"So I think it's possible that Woolworth's was only an excuse. I want to know where the girl was really going. She may have let slip something. If so, I feel Miss Marple's the person to get it out of these girls. I'd say she knows a thing or two about girls—more than I do. And, anyway, they'd be scared of the police."

"It sounds to me the kind of village domestic problem that is right up Miss Marple's street. She's very sharp, you know."

The Superintendent smiled. He said:

"I'll say you're right. Nothing much gets past her." Miss Marple looked up at their approach and welcomed them eagerly. She listened to the Superintendent's request and at once acquiesced.

"I should like to help you very much, Superintendent, and I think that perhaps I *could* be of some use. What with the Sunday School, you know, and the Brownies, and our Guides, and the Orphanage quite near—I'm on the committee, you know, and often run in to have a little talk with Matron—and then *servants*—I usually have very young maids. Oh, yes, I've quite a lot of experience in when a girl is speaking the truth and when she is holding something back."

"In fact, you're an expert," said Sir Henry.

Miss Marple flashed him a reproachful glance and said:

"Oh, *please* don't laugh at me, Sir Henry."

"I shouldn't dream of laughing at you. You've had the laugh of me too many times."

"One does see so much evil in a village," murmured Miss Marple in an explanatory voice.

"By the way," said Sir Henry, "I've cleared up one point you asked me about. The Superintendent tells me that there were nail clippings in Ruby's wastepaper basket."

Miss Marple said thoughtfully:

"There were? Then that's that. . . ."

"Why did you want to know, Miss Marple?" asked the Superintendent.

Miss Marple said:

"It was one of the things that—well, that seemed *wrong* when I looked at the body. The hands were wrong, somehow, and I couldn't at first think *why*. Then I realized that girls who are very much made-up, and all that, usually have very long fingernails. Of course, I know that girls everywhere do bite their nails—it's one of those habits that are very hard to break oneself of. But vanity often does a lot to help. Still, I presumed that this girl *hadn't* cured herself. And then the little boy—Peter, you know—he said something which showed that her nails *had* been long, only she caught one and broke it. So then, of course, she might have trimmed off the rest to make an even appearance, and I asked about clippings and Sir Henry said he'd find out."

Sir Henry remarked:

"You said just now, '*one* of the things that seemed wrong when you looked at the body.' Was there something else?"

Miss Marple nodded vigorously.

"Oh yes!" she said. "There was the dress. The dress was *all* wrong."

Both men looked at her curiously.

"Now why?" said Sir Henry.

"Well, you see, it was an old dress. Josie said so, definitely, and I could see for myself that it was shabby and rather worn. Now that's all wrong."

"I don't see why."

Miss Marple got a little pink.

"Well, the idea is, isn't it, that Ruby Keene changed her dress and went off to meet someone on whom she presumably had what my young nephews call a 'crush'?"

The Superintendent's eyes twinkled a little.

"That's the theory. She'd got a date with someone—a boy friend, as the saying goes."

"Then why," demanded Miss Marple, "was she wearing an old dress?"

The Superintendent scratched his head thoughtfully. He said:

"I see your point. You think she'd wear a new one?"

"I think she'd wear her best dress. Girls do."

Sir Henry interposed.

"Yes, but look here, Miss Marple. Suppose she was going outside to this *rendezvous*. Going in an open car, perhaps, or walking in some rough going. Then she'd not want to risk messing a new frock and she'd put on an old one."

"That would be the sensible thing to do," agreed the Superintendent.

Miss Marple turned on him. She spoke with animation.

"The sensible thing to do would be to change into trousers and a pullover, or into tweeds. That, of course (I don't want to be snobbish, but I'm afraid it's unavoidable), that's what a girl of—of our class would do.

"A well-bred girl," continued Miss Marple, warming to her subject, "is always very particular to wear the right clothes for the right occasion. I mean, however hot the day was, a well-bred girl would never turn up at a point-to-point in a silk flowered frock."

"And the correct wear to meet a lover?" demanded Sir Henry.

"If she were meeting him inside the hotel or somewhere where evening dress was worn, she'd wear her best evening frock, of course—but *outside* she'd feel she'd look ridiculous in evening dress and she'd wear her most attractive sportswear."

"Granted, Fashion Queen, but the girl Ruby—" Miss Marple said:

"Ruby, of course, wasn't—well, to put it bluntly—Ruby *wasn't* a lady. She belonged to the class that wear their best clothes however unsuitable to the occasion. Last year, you know, we had a picnic outing at Scrantor Rocks. You'd be surprised at the unsuitable clothes the girls wore. Foulard dresses and patent shoes and quite elaborate hats, some of them. For climbing about over rocks and in gorse and heather. And the young men in their best suits. Of course, hiking's different again. That's practically a uniform—and girls don't seem to realize that shorts are very unbecoming unless they are very slender."

The Superintendent said slowly:

"And you think that Ruby Keene—?"

"I think that she'd have kept on the frock she was wearing—her best pink one. She'd only have changed it if she'd had something newer still."

Superintendent Harper said:

"And what's your explanation, Miss Marple?"

Miss Marple said:

"I haven't got one—yet. But I can't help feeling that it's important. . . ."

III

Inside the wire cage, the tennis lesson that Raymond Starr was giving had come to an end.

A stout middle-aged woman uttered a few appreciative squeaks, picked up a sky-blue cardigan and went off towards the hotel.

Raymond called out a few gay words after her.

Then he turned towards the bench where the three onlookers were sitting. The balls dangled in a net in his hand, his racquet was under one arm. The gay, laughing expression on his face was wiped off as though by a sponge from a slate. He looked tired and worried.

Coming towards them, he said: "*That's* over."

Then the smile broke out again, that charming, boyish, expressive smile that went so harmoniously with his suntanned face and dark lithe grace.

Sir Henry found himself wondering how old the man was. Twenty-five, thirty, thirty-five? It was impossible to say.

Raymond said, shaking his head a little:

"*She*'ll never be able to play, you know."

"All this must be very boring for you," said Miss Marple.

Raymond said simply:

"It is, sometimes. Especially at the end of the summer. For a time the thought of the pay buoys you up, but even that fails to stimulate imagination in the end!"

Superintendent Harper got up. He said abruptly:

"I'll call for you in half an hour's time, Miss Marple, if that will be all right?"

"Perfectly, thank you. I shall be ready."

Harper went off. Raymond stood looking after him. Then he said: "Mind if I sit here for a bit?"

"Do," said Sir Henry. "Have a cigarette?" He offered his case, wondering as he did so why he had a slight feeling of prejudice against Raymond Starr. Was it simply because he was a professional tennis coach and dancer? If so, it wasn't the tennis—it was the dancing. The English, Sir Henry decided, had a distrust for any man who danced too well! This fellow moved with too much grace! Ramon—Raymond—which was his name? Abruptly, he asked the question.

The other seemed amused.

"Ramon was my original professional name. Ramon and Josie—Spanish effect, you know. Then there was rather a prejudice against foreigners—so I became Raymond—very British—"

Miss Marple said:

"And is your real name something quite different?"

He smiled at her.

"Actually my real name is Ramon. I had an Argentine grandmother, you see—" (And that accounts for that swing from the hips, thought Sir Henry parenthetically.) "But my first name is Thomas. Painfully prosaic."

He turned to Sir Henry.

"You come from Devonshire, don't you, sir? From Stane? My people lived down that way. At Alsmonston."

Sir Henry's face lit up.

"Are you one of the Alsmonston Starrs? I didn't realize that."

"No—I don't suppose you would."

There was a slight bitterness in his voice.

Sir Henry said awkwardly:

"Bad luck—er—all that."

"The place being sold up after it had been in the family for three hundred years? Yes, it was rather. Still, our kind have to go, I suppose. We've outlived our usefulness. My elder brother went to

New York. He's in publishing—doing well. The rest of us are scattered up and down the earth. I'll say it's hard to get a job nowadays when you've nothing to say for yourself except that you've had a public-school education! Sometimes, if you're lucky, you get taken on as a reception clerk at an hotel. The tie and the manner are an asset there. The only job I could get was showman in a plumbing establishment. Selling superb peach and lemon-coloured porcelain baths. Enormous showrooms, but as I never knew the price of the damned things or how soon we could deliver them—I got fired.

"The only things I *could* do were dance and play tennis. I got taken on at an hotel on the Riviera. Good pickings there. I suppose I was doing well. Then I overheard an old Colonel, real old Colonel, incredibly ancient, British to the backbone and always talking about Poona. He went up to the manager and said at the top of his voice:

" 'Where's the *gigolo?* I want to get hold of the *gigolo.* My wife and daughter want to dance, yer know. Where is the feller? What does he sting yer for? It's the *gigolo* I want.' "

Raymond went on:

"Silly to mind—but I did. I chucked it. Came here. Less pay but pleasanter work. Mostly teaching tennis to rotund women who will never, never, never be able to play. That and dancing with the neglected wallflower daughters of rich clients. Oh well, it's life, I suppose. Excuse today's hard-luck story!"

He laughed. His teeth flashed out white, his eyes crinkled up at the corners. He looked suddenly healthy and happy and very much alive.

Sir Henry said:

"I'm glad to have a chat with you. I've been wanting to talk with you."

"About Ruby Keene? I can't help you, you know. I don't know who killed her. I knew very little about her. She didn't confide in me."

Miss Marple said: "Did you like her?"

"Not particularly. I didn't dislike her."

His voice was careless, uninterested.

Sir Henry said:

"So you've no suggestions to offer?"

"I'm afraid not . . . I'd have told Harper if I had. It just seems to me one of those things! Petty, sordid little crime—no clues, no motive."

"Two people had a motive," said Miss Marple.

Sir Henry looked at her sharply.

"Really?" Raymond looked surprised.

Miss Marple looked insistently at Sir Henry and he said rather unwillingly:

"Her death probably benefits Mrs. Jefferson and Mr. Gaskell to the amount of fifty thousand pounds."

"What?" Raymond looked really startled—more than startled—upset. "Oh, but that's absurd—absolutely absurd—Mrs. Jefferson—neither of them—could have had anything to do with it. It would be incredible to think of such a thing."

Miss Marple coughed. She said gently:

"I'm afraid, you know, you're rather an idealist."

"I?" he laughed. "Not me! I'm a hard-boiled cynic."

"Money," said Miss Marple, "is a very powerful motive."

"Perhaps," Raymond said hotly. "But that either of those two would strangle a girl in cold blood—" He shook his head.

Then he got up.

"Here's Mrs. Jefferson now. Come for her lesson. She's late." His voice sounded amused. "Ten minutes late!"

Adelaide Jefferson and Hugo McLean were walking rapidly down the path towards them.

With a smiling apology for her lateness, Addie Jefferson went on to the court. McLean sat down on the bench. After a polite inquiry whether Miss Marple minded a pipe, he lit it and puffed for some minutes in silence, watching critically the two white figures about the tennis court.

He said at last:

"Can't see what Addie wants to have lessons for. Have a game, yes. No one enjoys it better than I do. But why *lessons?*"

"Wants to improve her game," said Sir Henry.

"She's not a bad player," said Hugo. "Good enough, at all events. Dash it all, she isn't aiming to play at Wimbledon."

He was silent for a minute or two. Then he said:

"Who *is* this Raymond fellow? Where do they come from, these pros? Fellow looks like a dago to me."

"He's one of the Devonshire Starrs," said Sir Henry.

"What? Not really?"

Sir Henry nodded. It was clear that this news was unpleasing to Hugo McLean. He scowled more than ever.

He said: "Don't know why Addie sent for *me*. She seems not to have turned a hair over this business! Never looked better. Why send for me?"

Sir Henry asked with some curiosity:

"When did she send for you?"

"Oh—er—when all this happened."

"How did you hear? Telephone or telegram?"

"Telegram."

"As a matter of curiosity, when was it sent off?"

"Well—I don't know exactly."

"What time did you receive it?"

"I didn't exactly receive it. It was telephoned on to me—as a matter of fact."

"Why, where were you?"

"Fact is, I'd left London the afternoon before. I was staying at Danebury Head."

"What—quite near here?"

"Yes, rather funny, wasn't it? Got the message when I got in from a round of golf and came over here at once."

Miss Marple gazed at him thoughtfully. He looked hot and uncomfortable. She said: "I've heard it's very pleasant at Danebury Head, and not very expensive."

"No, it's not expensive. I couldn't afford it if it was. It's a nice little place."

"We must drive over there one day," said Miss Marple.

"Eh? What? Oh—er—yes, I should." He got up. "Better take some exercise—get an appetite."

He walked away stiffly.

"Women," said Sir Henry, "treat their devoted admirers very badly."

Miss Marple smiled but made no answer.

"Does he strike you as rather a dull dog?" asked Sir Henry. "I'd be interested to know."

"A little limited in his ideas, perhaps," said Miss Marple. "But with possibilities, I think—oh, definitely possibilities."

Sir Henry in his turn got up.

"It's time for me to go and do my stuff. I see Mrs. Bantry is on her way to keep you company."

IV

Mrs. Bantry arrived breathless and sat down with a gasp.

She said:

"I've been talking to chambermaids. But it isn't any good. I haven't found out a thing more! Do you think that girl can really have been carrying on with someone without everybody in the hotel knowing all about it?"

"That's a very interesting point, dear. I should say, definitely *not. Somebody* knows, depend upon it, if it's true! But she must have been very clever about it."

Mrs. Bantry's attention had strayed to the tennis court. She said approvingly:

"Addie's tennis is coming on a lot. Attractive young man, that tennis pro. Addie's looking quite nice-looking. She's still an attractive woman—I shouldn't be at all surprised if she married again."

"She'll be a rich woman, too, when Mr. Jefferson dies," said Miss Marple.

"Oh, don't always have such a nasty mind, Jane! Why haven't you solved this mystery yet? We don't seem to be getting on at all. I thought you'd know *at once*." Mrs. Bantry's tone held reproach.

"No, no, dear. I didn't know at once—not for some time."

Mrs. Bantry turned startled and incredulous eyes on her.

"You mean you know *now* who killed Ruby Keene?"

"Oh yes," said Miss Marple, "I know *that!*"

"But Jane, who is it? Tell me at once."

Miss Marple shook her head very firmly and pursed up her lips.

"I'm sorry, Dolly, but that wouldn't do at all."

"Why wouldn't it do?"

"Because you're so indiscreet. You would go round telling everyone—or, if you didn't tell, you'd *hint*."

"No, I wouldn't. I wouldn't tell a soul."

"People who use that phrase are always the last to live up to it. It's no good, dear. There's a long way to go yet. A great many things that are quite obscure. You remember when I was so against letting Mrs. Partridge collect for the Red Cross, and I couldn't say *why*. The reason was that her nose had twitched in just the same way that that maid of mine, Alice, twitched *her* nose when I sent her out to pay the books. Always paid them a shilling or so short, and said 'it could go on to the next week's account,' which, of course, was *exactly* what Mrs. Partridge did, only on a much larger scale. Seventy-five pounds it was *she* embezzled."

"Never mind Mrs. Partridge," said Mrs. Bantry.

"But I had to explain to you. And if you care I'll

give you a *hint*. The trouble in this case is that everybody has been much too *credulous* and *believing*. You simply cannot *afford* to believe everything that people tell you. When there's anything fishy about, I never believe anyone at all! You see, I know human nature so well."

Mrs. Bantry was silent for a minute or two. Then she said in a different tone of voice:

"I told you, didn't I, that I didn't see why I shouldn't enjoy myself over this case. A real murder in my own house! The sort of thing that will never happen again."

"I hope not," said Miss Marple.

"Well, so do I, really. Once is enough. But it's *my* murder, Jane; I want to enjoy myself over it."

Miss Marple shot a glance at her.

Mrs. Bantry said belligerently:

"Don't you believe that?"

Miss Marple said sweetly:

"Of course, Dolly, if you tell me so."

"Yes, but you never believe what people tell you, do you? You've just said so. Well, you're quite right." Mrs. Bantry's voice took on a sudden bitter note. She said: "I'm not altogether a fool. You may think, Jane, that I don't know what they're saying all over St. Mary Mead—all over the county! They're saying, one and all, that there's no smoke without fire, that if the girl was found in Arthur's library, then Arthur must know something about it. They're saying that the girl was Arthur's mistress—that she was his illegitimate daughter—that she was blackmailing him. They're saying anything that comes into their damned heads! And it will go on like that! Arthur won't realize it at first—he won't know what's wrong. He's such a dear old stupid that he'd never believe people would think things like that about him. He'll be cold-shouldered and looked at askance (whatever *that* means!) and it will dawn on him little by little and suddenly he'll be horrified and cut to the soul, and he'll fasten up like a clam and just *endure,* day after day, in misery.

"It's because of all that's going to happen to him that I've come here to ferret out every single thing about it that I can! This murder's *got* to be solved! If it isn't, then Arthur's whole life will be wrecked—and I won't have that happen. I won't! I won't! I won't!"

She paused for a minute and said:

"I *won't* have the dear old boy go through hell for something he didn't do. That's the only reason I came to Danemouth and left him alone at home—to find out the truth."

"I know, dear," said Miss Marple. "That's why I'm here too."

Fourteen

In a quiet hotel room Edwards was listening deferentially to Sir Henry Clithering.

"There are certain questions I would like to ask you, Edwards, but I want you first to understand quite clearly my position here. I was at one time Commissioner of Police at Scotland Yard. I am now retired into private life. Your master sent for me when this tragedy occurred. He begged me to use my skill and experience in order to find out the truth."

Sir Henry paused.

Edwards, his pale intelligent eyes on the other's face, inclined his head. He said: "Quite so, Sir Henry."

Clithering went on slowly and deliberately:

"In all police cases there is necessarily a lot of information that is held back. It is held back for various reasons—because it touches on a family skeleton, because it is considered to have no bearing on the case, because it would entail awkwardness and embarrassment to the parties concerned."

Again Edwards said:

"Quite so, Sir Henry."

"I expect, Edwards, that by now you appreciate quite clearly the main points of this business. The dead girl was on the point of becoming Mr.

Jefferson's adopted daughter. Two people had a motive in seeing that this should not happen. Those two people are Mr. Gaskell and Mrs. Jefferson."

The valet's eyes displayed a momentary gleam. He said: "May I ask if they are under suspicion, sir?"

"They are in no danger of arrest, if that is what you mean. But the police are bound to be suspicious of them and will continue to be so *until the matter is cleared up*."

"An unpleasant position for them, sir."

"Very unpleasant. Now to get at the truth one must have *all* the facts of the case. A lot depends, *must* depend, on the reactions, the words and gestures, of Mr. Jefferson and his family. How did they feel, what did they show, what things were said? I am asking you, Edwards, for inside information—the kind of inside information that only you are likely to have. You know your master's moods. From observation of them you probably know what caused them. I am asking this, not as a policeman, but as a friend of Mr. Jefferson's. That is to say, if anything you tell me is not, in my opinion, relevant to the case, I shall not pass it on to the police."

He paused. Edwards said quietly:

"I understand you, sir. You want me to speak quite frankly—to say things that in the ordinary course of events I should not say—and that, excuse me, sir, *you* wouldn't dream of listening to."

Sir Henry said:

"You're a very intelligent fellow, Edwards. That's exactly what I *do* mean."

Edwards was silent for a minute or two, then he began to speak.

"Of course I know Mr. Jefferson fairly well by now. I've been with him quite a number of years. And I see him in his 'off' moments, not only in his 'on' ones. Sometimes, sir, I've questioned in my own mind whether it's good for anyone to fight fate in the way Mr. Jefferson has fought. It's taken a terrible toll of him, sir. If, sometimes, he could have given way, been an unhappy, lonely, broken old man—well, it might have been better for him in the end. But he's too proud for that! He'll go down fighting—that's his motto.

"But that sort of thing leads, Sir Henry, to a lot of nervous reaction. He looks a good-tempered gentleman. I've seen him in violent rages when he could hardly speak for passion. And the one thing that roused him, sir, was deceit. . . ."

"Are you saying that for any particular reason, Edwards?"

"Yes, sir, I am. You asked me, sir, to speak quite frankly?"

"That is the idea."

"Well, then, Sir Henry, in my opinion the young woman that Mr. Jefferson was so taken up with wasn't worth it. She was, to put it bluntly, a common little piece. And she didn't care tuppence for Mr. Jefferson. All that play of affection and gratitude was so much poppycock. I don't say there was any harm in her—but she wasn't, by a long way, what Mr. Jefferson thought her. It was funny, that, sir, for Mr. Jefferson was a shrewd gentleman; he wasn't often deceived over people. But there, a gentleman isn't himself in his judgment when it comes to a young woman being in question. Young Mrs. Jefferson, you see, whom he'd always depended upon a lot for sympathy, had changed a good deal this summer. He noticed it and he felt it badly. He was fond of her, you see. Mr. Mark he never liked much."

Sir Henry interjected:

"And yet he had him with him constantly?"

"Yes, but that was for Miss Rosamund's sake. Mrs. Gaskell that was. She was the apple of his eye. He adored her. Mr. Mark was Miss Rosamund's husband. He always thought of him like that."

"Supposing Mr. Mark had married someone else?"

"Mr. Jefferson, sir, would have been furious."

Sir Henry raised his eyebrows. "As much as that?"

"He wouldn't have shown it, but that's what it would have been."

"And if Mrs. Jefferson had married again?"

"Mr. Jefferson wouldn't have liked that either, sir."

"Please go on, Edwards."

"I was saying, sir, that Mr. Jefferson fell for this young woman. I've often seen it happen with the gentlemen I've been with. Comes over them like a kind of disease. They want to protect the girl, and shield her, and shower benefits upon her—and nine times out of ten the girl is very well able to look after herself and has a good eye to the main chance."

"So you think Ruby Keene was a schemer?"

"Well, Sir Henry, she was quite inexperienced, being so young, but she had the makings of a very fine schemer indeed when she'd once got well into her swing, so to speak! In another five years she'd have been an expert at the game!"

Sir Henry said:

"I'm glad to have your opinion of her. It's valuable. Now do you recall any incident in which this matter was discussed between Mr. Jefferson and his family?"

"There was very little discussion, sir. Mr. Jefferson announced what he had in mind and stifled any protests. That is, he shut up Mr. Mark, who was a bit outspoken. Mrs. Jefferson didn't say much—she's a quiet lady—only urged him not to do anything in a great hurry."

Sir Henry nodded.

"Anything else? What was the girl's attitude?"

With marked distaste the valet said:

"I should describe it, sir, as jubilant."

"Ah—jubilant, you say? You had no reason to believe, Edwards, that"—he sought about for a phrase suitable to Edwards—"that—er—her affections were engaged elsewhere?"

"Mr. Jefferson was not proposing marriage, sir. He was going to adopt her."

"Cut out the 'elsewhere' and let the question stand."

The valet said slowly: "There *was* one incident, sir. I happened to be a witness of it."

"That is gratifying. Tell me."

"There is probably nothing in it, sir. It was just that one day the young woman, chancing to open her handbag, a small snapshot fell out. Mr. Jefferson pounced on it and said: 'Hallo, Kitten, who's this, eh?'

"It was a snapshot, sir, of a young man, a dark young man with rather untidy hair and his tie very badly arranged.

"Miss Keene pretended that she didn't know anything about it. She said: 'I've no idea, Jeffie. No idea at all. I don't know how it could have got into my bag. *I* didn't put it there!'

"Now, Mr. Jefferson, sir, wasn't quite a fool. That story wasn't good enough. He looked angry, his brows came down heavy, and his voice was gruff when he said:

" 'Now then, Kitten, now then. *You* know who it is right enough.'

"She changed her tactics quick, sir. Looked frightened. She said: 'I do recognize him now. He comes here sometimes and I've danced with him. I don't know his name. The silly idiot must have stuffed his photo into my bag one day. These boys are too silly for anything!' She tossed her head and giggled and passed it off. But it wasn't a likely story, was it? And I don't think Mr. Jefferson quite believed it. He looked at her once or twice after that in a sharp way, and sometimes, if she'd been out, he asked her where she'd been."

Sir Henry said: "Have you ever seen the original of the photo about the hotel?"

"Not to my knowledge, sir. Of course, I am not much downstairs in the public departments."

Sir Henry nodded. He asked a few more questions, but Edwards could tell him nothing more.

II

In the police station at Danemouth, Superintendent Harper was interviewing Jessie Davis, Florence Small, Beatrice Henniker, Mary Price, and Lilian Ridgeway.

They were girls much of an age, differing slightly in mentality. They ranged from "county" to farmers' and shopkeepers' daughters. One and all they told the same story—Pamela Reeves had been just the same as usual, she had said nothing to any of them except that she was going to Woolworth's and would go home by a later bus.

In the corner of Superintendent Harper's office sat an elderly lady. The girls hardly noticed her. If they did, they may have wondered who she was. She was certainly no police matron. Possibly they assumed that she, like themselves, was a witness to be questioned.

The last girl was shown out. Superintendent Harper wiped his forehead and turned round to look at Miss Marple. His glance was inquiring, but not hopeful.

Miss Marple, however, spoke crisply.

"I'd like to speak to Florence Small."

The Superintendent's eyebrows rose, but he nodded and touched a bell. A constable appeared.

Harper said: "Florence Small."

The girl reappeared, ushered in by the constable. She was the daughter of a well-to-do farmer—a tall girl with fair hair, a rather foolish mouth, and frightened brown eyes. She was twisting her hands and looked nervous.

Superintendent Harper looked at Miss Marple, who nodded.

The Superintendent got up. He said:

"This lady will ask you some questions."

He went out, closing the door behind him.

Florence shot an uneasy glance at Miss Marple.

Her eyes looked rather like one of her father's calves.

Miss Marple said: "Sit down, Florence."

Florence Small sat down obediently. Unrecognized by herself, she felt suddenly more at home, less uneasy. The unfamiliar and terrorizing atmosphere of a police station was replaced by something more familiar, the accustomed tone of command of somebody whose business it was to give orders. Miss Marple said:

"You understand, Florence, that it's of the utmost importance that everything about poor Pamela's doings on the day of her death should be known?"

Florence murmured that she quite understood.

"And I'm sure you want to do your best to help?"

Florence's eyes were wary as she said, of course she did.

"To keep back any piece of information is a very serious offence," said Miss Marple.

The girl's fingers twisted nervously in her lap. She swallowed once or twice.

"I can make allowances," went on Miss Marple, "for the fact that you are naturally alarmed at being brought into contact with the police. You are afraid, too, that you may be blamed for not having spoken sooner. Possibly you are afraid that you may also be blamed for not stopping

Pamela at the time. But you've got to be a brave girl and make a clean breast of things. If you refuse to tell what you know now, it will be a very serious matter indeed—*very* serious—practically *perjury,* and for that, as you know, you can be sent to prison."

"I—I don't—"

Miss Marple said sharply:

"Now don't prevaricate, Florence! Tell me all about it at once! Pamela wasn't going to Woolworth's, was she?"

Florence licked her lips with a dry tongue and gazed imploringly at Miss Marple like a beast about to be slaughtered.

"Something to do with the films, wasn't it?" asked Miss Marple.

A look of intense relief mingled with awe passed over Florence's face. Her inhibitions left her. She gasped:

"Oh, *yes!*"

"I thought so," said Miss Marple. "Now I want all the details, please."

Words poured from Florence in a gush.

"Oh! I've been ever so worried. I promised Pam, you see, I'd never say a word to a soul. And then when she was found all burnt up in that car—oh! it was horrible and I thought I should *die*—I felt it was all my fault. I ought to have stopped her. Only I never thought, not for a minute, that it wasn't all right. And then I was asked if she'd been quite as usual that day and I said 'Yes' before I'd had time to think. And not having said anything then I didn't see how I could say anything later. And, after all, I didn't know anything—not really—only what Pam told me."

"What did Pam tell you?"

"It was as we were walking up the lane to the bus—on the way to the rally. She asked me if I could keep a secret, and I said 'Yes,' and she made me swear not to tell. She was going into Danemouth for a film test after the rally! She'd met a film producer—just back from Hollywood, he was. He wanted a certain type, and he told Pam she was just what he was looking for. He warned her, though, not to build on it. You couldn't tell, he said, not until you saw a person photographed. It might be no good at all. It was a kind of Bergner part, he said. You had to have someone quite young for it. A schoolgirl, it was, who changes places with a revue artist and has a wonderful career. Pam's acted in plays at school and she's awfully good. He said he could see she could act, but she'd have to have some intensive training. It wouldn't be all beer and skittles, he told her, it would be damned hard work. Did she think she could stick it?"

Florence Small stopped for breath. Miss Marple felt rather sick as she listened to the glib rehash of countless novels and screen stories. Pamela Reeves, like most other girls, would have been warned against talking to strangers—but the glamour of the films would obliterate all that.

"He was absolutely businesslike about it all," continued Florence. "Said if the test was successful she'd have a contract, and he said that as she was young and inexperienced she ought to let a lawyer look at it before she signed it. But she wasn't to pass on that *he'd* said that. He asked her if she'd have trouble with her parents, and Pam said she probably would, and he said: 'Well, of course, that's always a difficulty with anyone as young as you are, but I think if it was put to them that this was a wonderful chance that wouldn't happen once in a million times, they'd see reason.' But, anyway, he said, it wasn't any good going into that until they knew the result of the test. She mustn't be disappointed if it failed. He told her about Hollywood and about Vivien Leigh—how she'd suddenly taken London by storm—and how these sensational leaps into fame did happen. He himself had come back from America to work with the Lemville Studios and put some pep into the English film companies."

Miss Marple nodded.

Florence went on:

"So it was all arranged. Pam was to go into Danemouth after the rally and meet him at his hotel and he'd take her along to the studios (they'd got a small testing studio in Danemouth, he told her). She'd have her test and she could catch the bus home afterwards. She could say she'd been shopping, and he'd let her know the result of the test in a few days, and if it was favourable Mr. Harmsteiter, the boss, would come along and talk to her parents.

"Well, of course, it sounded too wonderful! I was green with envy! Pam got through the rally without turning a hair—we always call her a regular poker face. Then, when she said she was going into Danemouth to Woolworth's she just winked at me.

"I saw her start off down the footpath." Florence began to cry. "I ought to have stopped her. I ought to have stopped her. I ought to have known a thing like that couldn't be true. I ought to have told someone. Oh dear, I wish I was *dead!*"

"There, there." Miss Marple patted her on the shoulder. "It's quite all right. No one will blame you. You've done the right thing in telling me."

She devoted some minutes to cheering the child up.

Five minutes later she was telling the story to Superintendent Harper. The latter looked very grim.

"The clever devil!" he said. "By God, I'll cook his goose for him. This puts rather a different aspect on things."

"Yes, it does."

Harper looked at her sideways.

"It doesn't surprise you?"

"I expected something of the kind."

Superintendent Harper said curiously:

"What put you on to this particular girl? They all looked scared to death and there wasn't a pin to choose between them as far as I could see."

Miss Marple said gently:

"You haven't had as much experience with girls telling lies as I have. Florence looked at you very straight, if you remember, and stood very rigid and just fidgeted with her feet like the others. But you didn't watch her as she went out of the door. I knew at once then that she'd got something to hide. They nearly always relax too soon. My little maid Janet always did. She'd explain quite convincingly that the mice had eaten the end of a cake and give herself away by smirking as she left the room."

"I'm very grateful to you," said Harper.

He added thoughtfully: "Lemville Studios, eh?"

Miss Marple said nothing. She rose to her feet.

"I'm afraid," she said, "I must hurry away. So glad to have been able to help you."

"Are you going back to the hotel?"

"Yes—to pack up. I must go back to St. Mary Mead as soon as possible. There's a lot for me to do there."

Fifteen

Miss Marple passed out through the french windows of her drawing room, tripped down her neat garden path, through a garden gate, in through the vicarage garden gate, across the vicarage garden, and up to the drawing room window, where she tapped gently on the pane.

The vicar was busy in his study composing his Sunday sermon, but the vicar's wife, who was young and pretty, was admiring the progress of her offspring across the hearthrug.

"Can I come in, Griselda?"

"Oh, do, Miss Marple. Just *look* at David! He gets so angry because he can only crawl in reverse. He wants to get to something and the more he tries the more he goes backwards into the coal box!"

"He's looking very bonny, Griselda."

"He's not bad, is he?" said the young mother, endeavouring to assume an indifferent manner. "Of course I don't *bother* with him much. All the books say a child should be left alone as much as possible."

"Very wise, dear," said Miss Marple. "Ahem, I came to ask if there was anything special you are collecting for at the moment."

The vicar's wife turned somewhat astonished eyes upon her.

"Oh, heaps of things," she said cheerfully. "There always are."

She ticked them off on her fingers.

"There's the Nave Restoration Fund, and St. Giles's Mission, and our Sale of Work next Wednesday, and the Unmarried Mothers, and a Boy Scouts' Outing, and the Needlework Guild, and the Bishop's Appeal for Deep Sea Fishermen."

"Any of them will do," said Miss Marple. "I thought I might make a little round—with a book, you know—if you would authorize me to do so."

"Are you up to something? I believe you are. Of course I authorize you. Make it the Sale of Work; it would be lovely to get some real money instead of those awful sachets and comic pen-wipers and depressing children's frocks and dusters all done up to look like dolls.

"I suppose," continued Griselda, accompanying her guest to the window, "you wouldn't like to tell me what it's all about?"

"Later, my dear," said Miss Marple, hurrying off.

With a sigh the young mother returned to the hearthrug and, by way of carrying out her principles of stern neglect, butted her son three times in the stomach so that he caught hold of her hair and pulled it with gleeful yells. Then they rolled over and over in a grand rough-and-tumble until the door opened and the vicarage maid announced to the most influential parishioner (who didn't like children):

"Missus is in here."

Whereupon Griselda sat up and tried to look dignified and more what a vicar's wife should be.

II

Miss Marple, clasping a small black book with pencilled entries in it, walked briskly along the village street until she came to the crossroads. Here she turned to the left and walked past the *Blue Boar* until she came to Chatsworth, alias "Mr. Booker's new house."

She turned in at the gate, walked up to the front door and knocked briskly.

The door was opened by the blonde young woman named Dinah Lee. She was less carefully made-up than usual, and in fact looked slightly dirty. She was wearing grey slacks and an emerald jumper.

"Good morning," said Miss Marple briskly and cheerfully. "May I just come in for a minute?"

She pressed forward as she spoke, so that Dinah Lee, who was somewhat taken aback at the call, had no time to make up her mind.

"Thank you so much," said Miss Marple, beaming amiably at her and sitting down rather gingerly on a "period" bamboo chair.

"Quite warm for the time of year, is it not?" went on Miss Marple, still exuding geniality.

"Yes, rather. Oh, quite," said Miss Lee.

At a loss how to deal with the situation, she opened a box and offered it to her guest. "Er—have a cigarette?"

"Thank you so much, but I don't smoke. I just called, you know, to see if I could enlist your help for our Sale of Work next week."

"Sale of Work?" said Dinah Lee, as one who repeats a phrase in a foreign language.

"At the vicarage," said Miss Marple. "Next Wednesday."

"Oh!" Miss Lee's mouth fell open. "I'm afraid I couldn't—"

"Not even a small subscription—half a crown perhaps?"

Miss Marple exhibited her little book.

"Oh—er—well, yes, I dare say I could manage that."

The girl looked relieved and turned to hunt in her handbag.

Miss Marple's sharp eyes were looking round the room.

She said:

"I see you've no hearthrug in front of the fire."

Dinah Lee turned round and stared at her. She could not but be aware of the very keen scrutiny the old lady was giving her, but it aroused in her no other emotion than slight annoyance. Miss Marple recognized that. She said:

"It's rather dangerous, you know. Sparks fly out and mark the carpet."

"Funny old Tabby," thought Dinah, but she said quite amiably if somewhat vaguely:

"There used to be one. I don't know where it's got to."

"I suppose," said Miss Marple, "it was the fluffy, woolly kind?"

"Sheep," said Dinah. "That's what it looked like."

She was amused now. An eccentric old bean, this.

She held out a half crown. "Here you are," she said.

"Oh, thank you, my dear."

Miss Marple took it and opened the little book.

"Er—what name shall I write down?"

Dinah's eyes grew suddenly hard and contemptuous.

"Nosey old cat," she thought, "that's all she came for—prying around for scandal!"

She said clearly and with malicious pleasure:

"Miss Dinah Lee."

Miss Marple looked at her steadily.

She said:

"This is Mr. Basil Blake's cottage, isn't it?"

"Yes, and *I*'m Miss Dinah Lee!"

Her voice rang out challengingly, her head went back, her blue eyes flashed.

Very steadily Miss Marple looked at her. She said:

"Will you allow me to give you some advice, even though you may consider it impertinent?"

"I *shall* consider it impertinent. You had better say nothing."

"Nevertheless," said Miss Marple, "I am going to speak. I want to advise you, very strongly, not to continue using your maiden name in the village."

Dinah stared at her. She said:

"What—what do you mean?"

Miss Marple said earnestly:

"In a very short time you may need all the sympathy and goodwill you can find. It will be important to your husband, too, that he shall be thought well of. There is a prejudice in old-fashioned country districts against people living together who are not married. It has amused you both, I dare say, to pretend that that is what you are doing. It kept people away, so that you weren't bothered with what I expect you would call 'old frumps.' Nevertheless, old frumps have their uses."

Dinah demanded:

"How did you know we are married?"

Miss Marple smiled a deprecating smile.

"Oh, my dear," she said.

Dinah persisted.

"No, but how *did* you know? You didn't—you didn't go to Somerset House?"

A momentary flicker showed in Miss Marple's eyes.

"Somerset House? Oh, no. But it was quite easy to *guess*. Everything, you know, gets round in a village. The—er—the kind of quarrels you have—typical of early days of marriage. Quite—*quite* unlike an illicit relationship. It has been said, you know (and, I think, quite truly), that you can only really get under anybody's skin if you are married to them. When there is no—no *legal* bond, people are much more careful, they have to keep assuring themselves how happy and halcyon everything is. They have, you see, to *justify* themselves. They dare not quarrel! Married people, I have noticed, quite enjoy their battles and the—er—appropriate reconciliations."

She paused, twinkling benignly.

"Well, I—" Dinah stopped and laughed. She sat down and lit a cigarette. "You're absolutely marvellous!" she said.

Then she went on: "But why do you want us to own up and admit to respectability?"

Miss Marple's face was grave. She said:

"Because, any minute now, *your husband may be arrested for murder.*"

III

For several moments Dinah stared at her. Then she said incredulously:

"Basil? Murder? Are you joking?"

"No, indeed. Haven't you seen the papers?"

Dinah caught her breath.

"You mean—that girl at the Majestic Hotel. Do you mean they suspect Basil of killing her?"

"Yes."

"But it's nonsense!"

There was the whir of a car outside, the bang of a gate. Basil Blake flung open the door and came in, carrying some bottles. He said:

"Got the gin and the vermouth. Did you—?"

He stopped and turned incredulous eyes on the prim, erect visitor.

Dinah burst out breathlessly:

"Is she mad? She says you're going to be arrested for the murder of that girl Ruby Keene."

"Oh, God!" said Basil Blake. The bottles dropped from his arms on to the sofa. He reeled to a chair and dropped down in it and buried his face in his hands. He repeated: "Oh, my God! Oh, my God!"

Dinah darted over to him. She caught his shoulders.

"Basil, look at me! It isn't true! I know it isn't true! I don't believe it for a moment!"

His hand went up and gripped hers.

"Bless you, darling."

"But why should they think—You didn't even *know* her, did you?"

"Oh, yes, he knew her," said Miss Marple.

Basil said fiercely:

"Be quiet, you old hag. Listen, Dinah darling, I hardly knew her at all. Just ran across her once or twice at the Majestic. That's all, I swear that's all."

Dinah said, bewildered:

"I don't understand. Why should anyone suspect you, then?"

Basil groaned. He put his hands over his eyes and rocked to and fro.

Miss Marple said:

"What did you do with the hearthrug?"

His reply came mechanically:

"I put it in the dustbin."

Miss Marple clucked her tongue vexedly.

"That was stupid—very stupid. People don't put good hearthrugs in dustbins. It had spangles in it from her dress, I suppose?"

"Yes, I couldn't get them out."

Dinah cried: "But what are you both talking about?"

Basil said sullenly:

"Ask her. She seems to know all about it."

"I'll tell you what I think happened, if you like," said Miss Marple. "You can correct me, Mr. Blake, if I go wrong. I think that after having had a violent quarrel with your wife at a party and after having had, perhaps, rather too much—er— to drink, you drove down here. I don't know what time you arrived—"

Basil Blake said sullenly:

"About two in the morning. I meant to go up to town first, then when I got to the suburbs I changed my mind. I thought Dinah might come down here after me. So I drove down here. The place was all dark. I opened the door and turned on the light and I saw—and I saw—"

He gulped and stopped. Miss Marple went on:

"You saw a girl lying on the hearthrug—a girl in a white evening dress—strangled. I don't know whether you recognized her then—"

Basil Blake shook his head violently.

"I couldn't look at her after the first glance— her face was all blue—swollen. She'd been dead some time and she was *there*—in *my* room!"

He shuddered.

Miss Marple said gently:

"You weren't, of course, quite yourself. You were in a fuddled state and your nerves are not good. You were, I think, panic-stricken. You didn't know what to do—"

"I thought Dinah might turn up any minute. And she'd find me there with a dead body—a girl's dead body—and she'd think I'd killed her. Then I got an idea—it seemed, I don't know why, a good idea at the time—I thought: I'll put her in old Bantry's library. Damned pompous old stick, always looking down his nose, sneering at me as artistic and effeminate. Serve the pompous old brute right, I thought. He'll look a fool when a dead lovely is found on his hearthrug." He added, with a pathetic eagerness to explain: "I was a bit drunk, you know, at the time. It really seemed positively *amusing* to me. Old Bantry with a dead blonde."

"Yes, yes," said Miss Marple. "Little Tommy Bond had very much the same idea. Rather a sensitive boy with an inferiority complex, he said teacher was always picking on him. He put a frog in the clock and it jumped out at her.

"You were just the same," went on Miss Marple, "only of course, bodies are more serious matters than frogs."

Basil groaned again.

"By the morning I'd sobered up. I realized what I'd done. I was scared stiff. And then the police came here—another damned pompous ass of a Chief Constable. I was scared of him—and the only way I could hide it was by being abominably rude. In the middle of it all Dinah drove up."

Dinah looked out of the window.

She said:

"There's a car driving up now . . . there are men in it."

"The police, I think," said Miss Marple.

Basil Blake got up. Suddenly he became quite calm and resolute. He even smiled. He said:

"So I'm for it, am I? All right, Dinah sweet, keep your head. Get on to old Sims—he's the family lawyer—and go to Mother and tell her everything about our marriage. She won't bite. And don't worry. *I didn't do it.* So it's bound to be all right, see, sweetheart?"

There was a tap on the cottage door. Basil called "Come in." Inspector Slack entered with another man. He said:

"Mr. Basil Blake?"

"Yes."

"I have a warrant here for your arrest on the charge of murdering Ruby Keene on the night of September 21st last. I warn you that anything you say may be used at your trial. You will please accompany me now. Full facilities will be given you for communicating with your solicitor."

Basil nodded.

He looked at Dinah, but did not touch her. He said:

"So long, Dinah."

"Cool customer," thought Inspector Slack.

He acknowledged the presence of Miss Marple with a half bow and a "Good morning," and thought to himself:

"Smart old Pussy, *she's* on to it! Good job we've got that hearthrug. That and finding out from the car-park man at the studio that he left that party at *eleven* instead of midnight. Don't think those friends of his meant to commit perjury. They were bottled and Blake told 'em firmly the next day it was twelve o'clock when he left and they believed him. Well, *his* goose is cooked good and proper! Mental, I expect! Broadmoor, not hanging. First the Reeves kid, probably strangled her, drove her out to the quarry, walked back into Danemouth, picked up his own car in some side lane, drove to this party, then back to Danemouth, brought Ruby Keene out here, strangled her, put her in old Bantry's library, then probably got the wind up about the car in the quarry, drove there, set it on fire, and got back here. Mad—sex and blood lust—lucky *this* girl's escaped. What they call recurring mania, I expect."

Alone with Miss Marple, Dinah Blake turned to her. She said:

"I don't know who you are, but you've got to understand this—*Basil didn't do it.*"

Miss Marple said:

"I know he didn't. I know who *did* do it. But it's not going to be easy to prove. I've an idea that something you said—just now—may help. It gave me an idea—the *connection* I'd been trying to find—now what *was* it?"

Sixteen

"I'm home, Arthur!" declared Mrs. Bantry, announcing the fact like a Royal Proclamation as she flung open the study door.

Colonel Bantry immediately jumped up, kissed his wife, and declared heartily: "Well, well, that's splendid!"

The words were unimpeachable, the manner very well done, but an affectionate wife of as many years' standing as Mrs. Bantry was not deceived. She said immediately:

"Is anything the matter?"

"No, of course not, Dolly. What should be the matter?"

"Oh, I don't know," said Mrs. Bantry vaguely. "Things are so queer, aren't they?"

She threw off her coat as she spoke and Colonel Bantry picked it up as carefully and laid it across the back of the sofa.

All exactly as usual—yet not as usual. Her husband, Mrs. Bantry thought, seemed to have shrunk. He looked thinner, stooped more; they were pouches under his eyes and those eyes were not ready to meet hers.

He went on to say, still with that affectation of cheerfulness:

"Well, how did you enjoy your time at Danemouth?"

"Oh! it was great fun. You ought to have come, Arthur."

"Couldn't get away, my dear. Lot of things to attend to here."

"Still, I think the change would have done you good. And you like the Jeffersons?"

"Yes, yes, poor fellow. Nice chap. All very sad."

"What have you been doing with yourself since I've been away?"

"Oh, nothing much. Been over the farms, you know. Agreed that Anderson shall have a new roof—can't patch it up any longer."

"How did the Radfordshire Council meeting go?"

"I—well—as a matter of fact I didn't go."

"Didn't *go?* But you were taking the chair?"

"Well, as a matter of fact, Dolly—seems there was some mistake about that. Asked me if I'd mind if Thompson took it instead."

"I *see*," said Mrs. Bantry.

She peeled off a glove and threw it deliberately into the wastepaper basket. Her husband went to retrieve it, and she stopped him, saying sharply:

"Leave it. I hate gloves."

Colonel Bantry glanced at her uneasily.

Mrs. Bantry said sternly:

"Did you go to dinner with the Duffs on Thursday?"

"Oh, that! It was put off. Their cook was ill."

"Stupid people," said Mrs. Bantry. She went on: "Did you go to the Naylors' yesterday?"

"I rang up and said I didn't feel up to it, hoped they'd excuse me. They quite understood."

"They did, did they?" said Mrs. Bantry grimly.

She sat down by the desk and absentmindedly picked up a pair of gardening scissors. With them she cut off the fingers, one by one, of her second glove.

"What *are* you doing, Dolly?"

"Feeling destructive," said Mrs. Bantry.

She got up. "Where shall we sit after dinner, Arthur? In the library?"

"Well—er—I don't think so—eh? Very nice in here—or the drawing room."

"I think," said Mrs. Bantry, "that we'll sit in the library!"

Her steady eye met his. Colonel Bantry drew himself up to his full height. A sparkle came into his eye.

He said:

"You're right, my dear. We'll sit in the library!"

II

Mrs. Bantry put down the telephone receiver with a sigh of annoyance. She had rung up twice, and each time the answer had been the same: Miss Marple was out.

Of a naturally impatient nature, Mrs. Bantry

was never one to acquiesce in defeat. She rang up in rapid succession the vicarage, Mrs. Price Ridley, Miss Hartnell, Miss Wetherby, and, as a last resource, the fishmonger who, by reason of his advantageous geographical position, usually knew where everybody was in the village.

The fishmonger was sorry, but he had not seen Miss Marple at all in the village that morning. She had not been her usual round.

"Where *can* the woman be?" demanded Mrs. Bantry impatiently aloud.

There was a deferential cough behind her. The discreet Lorrimer murmured:

"You were requiring Miss Marple, madam? I have just observed her approaching the house."

Mrs. Bantry rushed to the front door, flung it open, and greeted Miss Marple breathlessly:

"I've been trying to get you *everywhere*. Where have you been?" She glanced over her shoulder. Lorrimer had discreetly vanished. "Everything's *too* awful! People are beginning to cold-shoulder Arthur. He looks *years* older. We *must* do something, Jane. *You* must do something!"

Miss Marple said:

"You needn't worry, Dolly," in a rather peculiar voice.

Colonel Bantry appeared from the study door.

"Ah, Miss Marple. Good morning. Glad you've come. My wife's been ringing you up like a lunatic."

"I thought I'd better bring you the news," said Miss Marple, as she followed Mrs. Bantry into the study.

"News?"

"Basil Blake has just been arrested for the murder of Ruby Keene."

"Basil Blake?" cried the Colonel.

"But he didn't do it," said Miss Marple.

Colonel Bantry took no notice of this statement. It is doubtful if he even heard it.

"Do you mean to say he strangled that girl and then brought her along and put her in *my* library?"

"He put her in your library," said Miss Marple. "But he didn't kill her."

"Nonsense! If he put her in my library, of course he killed her! The two things go together."

"Not necessarily. He found her dead in his own cottage."

"A likely story," said the Colonel derisively. "If you find a body, why, you ring up the police— naturally—if you're an honest man."

"Ah," said Miss Marple, "but we haven't all got such iron nerves as you have, Colonel Bantry. You belong to the old school. This younger generation is different."

"Got no stamina," said the Colonel, repeating a well-worn opinion of his.

"Some of them," said Miss Marple, "have been through a bad time. I've heard a good deal about Basil. He did A.R.P. work, you know, when he was only eighteen. He went into a burning house and brought out four children, one after another. He went back for a dog, although they told him it wasn't safe. The building fell in on him. They got him out, but his chest was badly crushed and he had to lie in plaster for nearly a year and was ill for a long time after that. That's when he got interested in designing."

"Oh!" The Colonel coughed and blew his nose. "I—er—never knew that."

"He doesn't talk about it," said Miss Marple.

"Er—quite right. Proper spirit. Must be more in the young chap than I thought. Always thought he'd shirked the war, you know. Shows you ought to be careful in jumping to conclusions."

Colonel Bantry looked ashamed.

"But, all the same"—his indignation revived—"what did he mean trying to fasten a murder on *me?*"

"I don't think he saw it like that," said Miss Marple. "He thought of it more as a—as a joke. You see, he was rather under the influence of alcohol at the time."

"Bottled, was he?" said Colonel Bantry, with an Englishman's sympathy for alcoholic excess. "Oh, well, can't judge a fellow by what he does when he's drunk. When I was at Cambridge, I remember I put a certain utensil—well, well, never mind. Deuce of a row there was about it."

He chuckled, then checked himself sternly. He

235

looked piercingly at Miss Marple with eyes that were shrewd and appraising. He said: "*You* don't think he did the murder, eh?"

"I'm sure he didn't."

"And you think you know who did?"

Miss Marple nodded.

Mrs. Bantry, like an ecstatic Greek chorus, said: "Isn't she wonderful?" to an unhearing world.

"Well, who was it?"

Miss Marple said:

"I was going to ask you to help me. I think, if we went up to Somerset House we should have a very good idea."

Seventeen

Sir Henry's face was very grave.

He said:

"I don't like it."

"I am aware," said Miss Marple, "that it isn't what you call orthodox. But it *is* so important, isn't it, to be quite *sure*—'to make assurance doubly sure,' as Shakespeare has it. I think, if Mr. Jefferson would agree—?"

"What about Harper? Is he to be in on this?"

"It might be awkward for him to know too much. But there might be a hint from you. To watch certain persons—have them trailed, you know."

Sir Henry said slowly:

"Yes, that would meet the case. . . ."

II

Superintendent Harper looked piercingly at Sir Henry Clithering.

"Let's get this quite clear, sir. You're giving me a hint?"

Sir Henry said:

"I'm informing you of what my friend has just informed me—he didn't tell me in confidence— that he proposes to visit a solicitor in Danemouth tomorrow for the purpose of making a new will."

The Superintendent's bushy eyebrows drew downwards over his steady eyes. He said:

"Does Mr. Conway Jefferson propose to inform his son-in-law and daughter-in-law of that fact?"

"He intends to tell them about it this evening."

"I see."

The Superintendent tapped his desk with a penholder.

He repeated again: "I see. . . ."

Then the piercing eyes bored once more into the eyes of the other man. Harper said:

"So you're not satisfied with the case against Basil Blake?"

"Are you?"

The Superintendent's moustaches quivered. He said:

"Is Miss Marple?"

The two men looked at each other.

Then Harper said:

"You can leave it to me. I'll have men detailed. There will be no funny business, I can promise you that."

Sir Henry said:

"There is one more thing. You'd better see this."

He unfolded a slip of paper and pushed it across the table.

This time the Superintendent's calm deserted him. He whistled:

"So that's it, is it? That puts an entirely different

238

complexion on the matter. How did you come to dig up this?"

"Women," said Sir Henry, "are eternally interested in marriages."

"Especially," said the Superintendent, "elderly single women."

III

Conway Jefferson looked up as his friend entered.

His grim face relaxed into a smile.

He said:

"Well, I told 'em. They took it very well."

"What did you say?"

"Told 'em that, as Ruby was dead, I felt that the fifty thousand I'd originally left her should go to something that I could associate with her memory. It was to endow a hostel for young girls working as professional dancers in London. Damned silly way to leave your money— surprised they swallowed it. As though *I*'d do a thing like that!"

He added meditatively:

"You know, I made a fool of myself over that girl. Must be turning into a silly old man. I can see it now. She was a pretty kid—but most of what I saw in her I put there myself. I pretended she was another Rosamund. Same colouring, you know. But not the same heart or mind. Hand me that paper—rather an interesting bridge problem."

IV

Sir Henry went downstairs. He asked a question of the porter.

"Mr. Gaskell, sir? He's just gone off in his car. Had to go to London."

"Oh! I see. Is Mrs. Jefferson about?"

"Mrs. Jefferson, sir, has just gone up to bed."

Sir Henry looked into the lounge and through to the ballroom. In the lounge Hugo McLean was doing a crossword puzzle and frowning a good deal over it. In the ballroom Josie was smiling valiantly into the face of a stout, perspiring man as her nimble feet avoided his destructive tread. The stout man was clearly enjoying his dance. Raymond, graceful and weary, was dancing with an anaemic-looking girl with adenoids, dull brown hair, and an expensive and exceedingly unbecoming dress.

Sir Henry said under his breath:

"And so to bed," and went upstairs.

V

It was three o'clock. The wind had fallen, the moon was shining over the quiet sea.

In Conway Jefferson's room there was no sound except his own heavy breathing as he lay, half propped up on pillows.

There was no breeze to stir the curtains at the window, but they stirred . . . For a moment they parted, and a figure was silhouetted against the moonlight. Then they fell back into place. Everything was quiet again, but there was someone else inside the room.

Nearer and nearer to the bed the intruder stole. The deep breathing on the pillow did not relax.

There was no sound, or hardly any sound. A finger and thumb were ready to pick up a fold of skin, in the other hand the hypodermic was ready.

And then, suddenly, out of the shadows a hand came and closed over the hand that held the needle, the other arm held the figure in an iron grasp.

An unemotional voice, the voice of the law, said:

"No, you don't. I want that needle!"

The light switched on and from his pillows Conway Jefferson looked grimly at the murderer of Ruby Keene.

Eighteen

Sir Henry Clithering said:

"Speaking as Watson, I want to know your methods, Miss Marple."

Superintendent Harper said:

"*I*'d like to know what put you on to it first."

Colonel Melchett said:

"You've done it again, by Jove! I want to hear all about it from the beginning."

Miss Marple smoothed the puce silk of her best evening gown. She flushed and smiled and looked very self-conscious.

She said: "I'm afraid you'll think my 'methods,' as Sir Henry calls them, are terribly amateurish. The truth is, you see, that most people—and I don't exclude policemen—are far too trusting for this wicked world. They believe what is told them. I never do. I'm afraid I always like to prove a thing for myself."

"That is the scientific attitude," said Sir Henry.

"In this case," continued Miss Marple, "certain things were taken for granted from the first—instead of just confining oneself to the facts. The facts, as I noted them, were that the victim was quite young and that she bit her nails and that her teeth stuck out a little—as young girls' so often do if not corrected in time with a plate—(and children are very naughty about their plates and taking them out when their elders aren't looking).

"But that is wandering from the point. Where was I? Oh, yes, looking down at the dead girl and feeling sorry, because it is always sad to see a young life cut short, and thinking that whoever had done it was a very wicked person. Of course it was all very confusing her being found in Colonel Bantry's library, altogether too like a book to be *true*. In fact, it made the wrong pattern. It wasn't, you see, *meant,* which confused us a lot. The *real* idea had been to plant the body on poor young Basil Blake (a *much* more likely person), and his action in putting it in the Colonel's library delayed things considerably, and must have been a source of great annoyance to the *real* murderer.

"Originally, you see, Mr. Blake would have been the first object of suspicion. They'd have made inquiries at Danemouth, found he knew the girl, then found he had tied himself up with another girl, and they'd have assumed that Ruby came to blackmail him, or something like that, and that he'd strangled her in a fit of rage. Just an ordinary, sordid, what I call *nightclub* type of crime!

"But that, of course, *all went wrong,* and interest became focused much too soon on the Jefferson family—to the great annoyance of a *certain person.*

"As I've told you, I've got a very suspicious mind. My nephew Raymond tells me (in fun, of course, and quite affectionately) that I have a mind like a *sink*. He says that most Victorians have. All I can say is that the Victorians knew a good deal about human nature.

"As I say, having this rather insanitary—or surely *sanitary?*—mind, I looked at once at the *money* angle of it. Two people stood to benefit by this girl's death—you couldn't get away from that. Fifty thousand pounds is a lot of money—especially when you are in financial difficulties, as both these people were. Of course they both seemed very nice, agreeable people—they didn't seem *likely* people—but one never can tell, can one?

"Mrs. Jefferson, for instance—everyone liked her. But it did seem clear that she had become very restless that summer, and that she was tired of the life she led, completely dependent on her father-in-law. She knew, because the doctor had told her, that he couldn't live long—so *that* was all right—to put it callously—or it *would* have been all right if Ruby Keene hadn't come along. Mrs. Jefferson was passionately devoted to her son, and some women have a curious idea that crimes committed for the sake of their offspring are almost morally justified. I have come across that attitude once or twice in the village. 'Well, 'twas all for Daisy, you see, miss,' they say, and seem to think that that makes doubtful conduct quite all right. Very *lax* thinking.

"Mr. Mark Gaskell, of course, was a much more likely starter, if I may use such a sporting expression. He was a gambler and had not, I fancied, a very high moral code. But, for certain reasons, I was of the opinion that a *woman* was concerned in this crime.

"As I say, with my eye on motive, the money angle seemed *very* suggestive. It was annoying, therefore, to find that both these people had alibis for the time when Ruby Keene, according to the medical evidence, had met her death.

"But soon afterwards there came the discovery of the burnt-out car with Pamela Reeves's body in it, and then the whole thing leaped to the eye. The alibis, of course, were worthless.

"I now had two *halves* of the case, and both quite convincing, but they did not fit. There must *be* a connection, but I could not find it. The one person whom I *knew* to be concerned in the crime hadn't got a motive.

"It was stupid of me," said Miss Marple meditatively. "If it hadn't been for Dinah Lee I shouldn't have thought of it—the most obvious thing in the world. Somerset House! Marriage! It wasn't a question of only Mr. Gaskell or Mrs. Jefferson—there were the further possibilities of *marriage.* If either of those two was married, or even was *likely* to marry, *then the other party to the marriage contract was involved too.* Raymond, for instance, might think he had a pretty good chance of marrying a rich wife. He had been very assiduous to Mrs. Jefferson, and it was his charm, I think, that awoke her from her long widowhood. She had been quite content just being a daughter to Mr. Jefferson—like Ruth and Naomi—only Naomi, if you remember, took a lot of trouble to arrange a suitable marriage for Ruth.

"Besides Raymond there was Mr. McLean. She liked him very much and it seemed highly possible that she would marry him in the end. *He* wasn't well off—and he was not far from Danemouth on the night in question. So it seemed, didn't it," said Miss Marple, "as though *anyone* might have done it?

"But, of course, really, in my mind, I *knew.* You couldn't get away, could you, from those bitten nails?"

"Nails?" said Sir Henry. "But she tore her nail and cut the others."

"Nonsense," said Miss Marple. "*Bitten* nails and close *cut* nails are quite different! Nobody could mistake them who knew anything about girl's nails—very ugly, bitten nails, as I always tell the girls in my class. Those nails, you see, were a *fact.* And they could only mean one thing. *The body in Colonel Bantry's library wasn't Ruby Keene at all.*

"And that brings you straight to the one person who must be concerned. *Josie!* Josie identified the body. She knew, she *must* have known, that it

246

wasn't Ruby Keene's body. She said it was. She was puzzled, completely puzzled, at finding that body where it was. She practically betrayed that fact. Why? Because *she* knew, none better, where it ought to have been found! In Basil Blake's cottage. Who directed our attention to Basil? Josie, by saying to Raymond that Ruby might have been with the film man. And before that, by slipping a snapshot of him into Ruby's handbag. Who cherished such bitter anger against the dead girl that she couldn't hide it even when she looked down at her dead? Josie! Josie, who was shrewd, practical, hard as nails, and *all out for money.*

"That is what I meant about believing too readily. Nobody thought of disbelieving Josie's statement that the body was Ruby Keene's. Simply because it didn't seem at the time that she could have any motive for lying. Motive was always the difficulty—Josie was clearly involved, but Ruby's death seemed, if anything, contrary to her interests. It was not till Dinah Lee mentioned Somerset House that I got the connection.

"Marriage! If Josie and Mark Gaskell were actually married—then the whole thing was clear. As we know now, Mark and Josie were married a year ago. They were keeping it dark until Mr. Jefferson died.

"It was really quite interesting, you know, tracing out the course of events—seeing exactly how the plan had worked out. Complicated and yet simple. First of all the selection of the poor child, Pamela, the approach to her from the film angle. A screen test—of course the poor child couldn't resist it. Not when it was put up to her as plausibly as Mark Gaskell put it. She comes to the hotel, he is waiting for her, he takes her in by the side door and introduces her to Josie—one of their makeup experts! That poor child, it makes me quite sick to think of it! Sitting in Josie's bathroom while Josie bleaches her hair and makes up her face and varnishes her fingernails and toenails. During all this, the drug was given. In an ice cream soda, very likely. She goes off into a coma. I imagine that they put her into one of the empty rooms opposite—they were only cleaned once a week, remember.

"After dinner Mark Gaskell went out in his car—to the seafront, *he* said. That is when he took Pamela's body to the cottage dressed in one of Ruby's old dresses and arranged it on the hearthrug. She was still unconscious, but not dead, when he strangled her with the belt of the frock . . . Not nice, no—but I hope and pray she knew nothing about it. Really, I feel quite pleased to think of him being hanged . . . That must have been just after ten o'clock. Then he drove back at top speed and found the others in the lounge where Ruby Keene, *still alive,* was dancing her exhibition dance with Raymond.

"I should imagine that Josie had given Ruby instructions beforehand. Ruby was accustomed to doing what Josie told her. She was to change, go into Josie's room and wait. She, too, was drugged, probably in after-dinner coffee. She was yawning, remember, when she talked to young Bartlett.

"Josie came up later to 'look for her'—*but nobody but Josie went into Josie's room.* She probably finished the girl off then—with an injection, perhaps, or a blow on the back of the head. She went down, danced with Raymond, debated with the Jeffersons where Ruby could be, and finally went to bed. In the early hours of the morning she dressed the girl in Pamela's clothes, carried the body down the side stairs—she was a strong muscular young woman—fetched George Bartlett's car, drove two miles to the quarry, poured petrol over the car and set it alight. Then she walked back to the hotel, probably timing her arrival there for eight or nine o'clock—up early in her anxiety about Ruby!"

"An intricate plot," said Colonel Melchett.

"Not more intricate than the steps of a dance," said Miss Marple.

"I suppose not."

"She was very thorough," said Miss Marple. "She even foresaw the discrepancy of the nails. That's why she managed to break one of Ruby's nails on her shawl. It made an excuse for pretending that Ruby had clipped her nails close."

Harper said: "Yes, she thought of everything. And the only real proof you had, Miss Marple, was a schoolgirl's bitten nails."

"More than that," said Miss Marple. "People *will* talk too much. Mark Gaskell talked too much. He was speaking of Ruby and he said 'her teeth ran down her throat.' But the dead girl in Colonel Bantry's library had teeth that stuck *out.*"

Conway Jefferson said rather grimly:

"And was the last dramatic *finale* your idea, Miss Marple?"

Miss Marple confessed. "Well, it *was,* as a matter of fact. It's so nice to be *sure,* isn't it?"

"Sure is the word," said Conway Jefferson grimly.

"You see," said Miss Marple, "once Mark and Josie knew that you were going to make a new will, they'd *have* to do something. They'd already committed *two* murders on account of the money. So they might as well commit a third. Mark, of course, must be absolutely clear, so he went off to London and established an alibi by dining at a restaurant with friends and going on to a night club. Josie was to do the work. They still wanted Ruby's death to be put down to Basil's account, so Mr. Jefferson's death must be thought due to his heart failing. There was digitalin, so the Superintendent tells me, in the syringe. Any doctor would think death from heart trouble quite natural in the circumstances. Josie had loosened one of the stone balls on the balcony and she was going to let it crash down afterwards. His death would be put down to the shock of the noise."

Melchett said: "Ingenious devil."

Sir Henry said: "So the third death you spoke of was to be Conway Jefferson?"

Miss Marple shook her head.

"Oh no—I meant Basil Blake. They'd have got him hanged if they could."

"Or shut up in Broadmoor," said Sir Henry.

Conway Jefferson grunted. He said:

"Always knew Rosamund had married a rotter. Tried not to admit it to myself. She was damned fond of him. Fond of a murderer! Well, he'll hang as well as the woman. I'm glad he went to pieces and gave the show away."

Miss Marple said:

"She was always the strong character. It was her plan throughout. The irony of it is that she got the girl down here herself, never dreaming that she would take Mr. Jefferson's fancy and ruin all her own prospects."

Jefferson said:

"Poor lass. Poor little Ruby. . . ."

Adelaide Jefferson and Hugo McLean came in. Adelaide looked almost beautiful tonight. She came up to Conway Jefferson and laid a hand on his shoulder. She said, with a little catch in her breath:

"I want to tell you something, Jeff. At once. I'm going to marry Hugo."

Conway Jefferson looked up at her for a moment. He said gruffly:

"About time you married again. Congratulations to you both. By the way, Addie, I'm making a new will tomorrow."

She nodded. "Oh yes, I know."

Jefferson said:

"No, you don't. I'm settling ten thousand pounds on you. Everything else I have goes to Peter when I die. How does that suit you, my girl?"

"Oh, *Jeff!*" Her voice broke. "You're *wonderful!*"

"He's a nice lad. I'd like to see a good deal of him—in the time I've got left."

"Oh, you shall!"

"Got a great feeling for crime, Peter has," said Conway Jefferson meditatively. "Not only has he got the fingernail of the murdered girl—one of the murdered girls, anyway—but he was lucky enough to have a bit of Josie's shawl caught in with the nail. So he's got a souvenir of the murderess too! That makes him *very* happy!"

II

Hugo and Adelaide passed by the ballroom. Raymond came up to them.

Adelaide said, rather quickly:

"I must tell you my news. We're going to be married."

The smile on Raymond's face was perfect—a brave, pensive smile.

"I hope," he said, ignoring Hugo and gazing into her eyes, "that you will be very, very happy. . . ."

They passed on and Raymond stood looking after them.

"A nice woman," he said to himself. "A very nice woman. And she would have had money too. The trouble I took to mug up that bit about the Devonshire Starrs . . . Oh well, my luck's out. Dance, dance, little gentleman!"

And Raymond returned to the ballroom.

About the Author

Agatha Christie is the most widely published author of all time and in any language, outsold only by the Bible and Shakespeare. Her books have sold more than a billion copies in English and another billion in a hundred foreign languages. She is the author of eighty crime novels and short-story collections, nineteen plays, two memoirs, and six novels written under the name Mary Westmacott.

She first tried her hand at detective fiction while working in a hospital dispensary during World War I, creating the now legendary Hercule Poirot with her debut novel *The Mysterious Affair at Styles*. With *The Murder in the Vicarage*, published in 1930, she introduced another beloved sleuth, Miss Jane Marple. Additional series characters include the husband-and-wife crime-fighting team of Tommy and Tuppence Beresford, private investigator Parker Pyne, and Scotland Yard detectives Superintendent Battle and Inspector Japp.

Many of Christie's novels and short stories were adapted into plays, films, and television series. *The Mousetrap*, her most famous play of all, opened in 1952 and is the longest-running play in history. Among her best-known film adaptations are *Murder on the Orient Express*

(1974) and *Death on the Nile* (1978), with Albert Finney and Peter Ustinov playing Hercule Poirot, respectively. On the small screen Poirot has been most memorably portrayed by David Suchet, and Miss Marple by Joan Hickson and subsequently Geraldine McEwan and Julia McKenzie.

Christie was first married to Archibald Christie and then to archaeologist Sir Max Mallowan, whom she accompanied on expeditions to countries that would also serve as the settings for many of her novels. In 1971 she achieved one of Britain's highest honors when she was made a Dame of the British Empire. She died in 1976 at the age of eighty-five. Her one hundred and twentieth anniversary was celebrated around the world in 2010.

www.AgathaChristie.com

Center Point Publishing

600 Brooks Road • PO Box 1
Thorndike ME 04986-0001 USA

(207) 568-3717

US & Canada:
1 800 929-9108
www.centerpointlargeprint.com